"OH, SABRINA, WHAT YOU DO TO ME," COLIN MURMURED. . . .

Colin's hands strayed to Sabrina's waist. "Come here," he said, pulling her close. He kissed her, his stance firm and commanding, and as Sabrina melted against him, she began to tremble.

Each kiss was long and provocative, followed up at once with another one and then another that sent Sabrina's senses spinning.

"I'll never get enough of you!" he whispered.

And Sabrina didn't want him to. . . .

DIANA MORGAN is a pseudonym for a husband-and-wife writing team. Residents of New York City, they met in a phone booth at Columbia University, and have been together romantically and professionally ever since. Their previous Rapture Romances are *Amber Dreams*, *Emerald Dreams*, and *Crystal Dreams*.

Dear Reader:

We at Rapture Romance hope you will continue to enjoy our four books each month as much as we enjoy bringing them to you. Our commitment remains strong to giving you only the best, by well-known favorite authors and exciting new writers.

We've used the comments and opinions we've heard from *you*, the reader, to make our selections, so please keep writing to us. Your letters have already helped us bring you better books—the kind you want—and we appreciate and depend on them. Of course, we are always happy to forward mail to our authors—writers need to hear from their fans!

And don't miss any of the inside story on Rapture. To tell you about upcoming books, introduce you to the authors, and give you a behind-the-scenes look at romance publishing, we've started a *free* newsletter, *The Rapture Reader*. Just write to the address below, and we will be happy to send you each issue.

Happy reading!

The Editors
Rapture Romance
New American Library
1633 Broadway
New York, NY 10019

LADY IN FLIGHT

by
Diana Morgan

RAPTURE ROMANCE

NEW AMERICAN LIBRARY

PUBLISHER'S NOTE

This novel is a work of fiction. Names, characters, places, and incidents either are the product of the author's imagination or are used fictitiously, and any resemblance to actual persons, living or dead, events, or locales is entirely coincidental.

NAL BOOKS ARE AVAILABLE AT QUANTITY DISCOUNTS
WHEN USED TO PROMOTE PRODUCTS OR SERVICES.
FOR INFORMATION PLEASE WRITE TO PREMIUM MARKETING DIVISION,
NEW AMERICAN LIBRARY, 1633 BROADWAY,
NEW YORK, NEW YORK 10019.

Copyright © 1984 by Irene Goodman and Alex Kamoroff

SIGNET, SIGNET CLASSIC, MENTOR, PLUME, MERIDIAN
and NAL BOOKS are published by New American Library,
1633 Broadway, New York, New York 10019

First Printing, June, 1984

1 2 3 4 5 6 7 8 9

PRINTED IN THE UNITED STATES OF AMERICA

To Robin,
editor par excellence

Chapter One

❧

The tall man had been hunched down for over fifteen minutes, his face only inches from the statue's derriere. At last he spoke. "Priceless," he said reverently. "Absolutely priceless."

Curious, Sabrina gazed at him from across her SoHo loft, a spacious room that was now filled with hazy smoke, lively chatter, and a crush of people. Ordinarily, nothing unusual happened at Sabrina's parties. But this was uncommon, even here. She frowned, wondering what on earth the man was doing, but his intense concentration offered no clues.

He started running his hands around her statue's torso as if he were searching for something. He was drawing a few curious stares and raised eyebrows, and at last Sabrina decided to question him delicately about what he was doing.

She downed the rest of her Singapore sling in one gulp and threaded her way lightly through the crowd. *Lady in Flight*, the life-size sculpture that had taken her six months to create, stood proudly in the center of the huge room. Everyone had stopped to admire it and to comment on its excellent chances at tomorrow's auction, but no one had examined it quite as intimately as this stranger was doing now. His nose still faced the *Lady's* limestone bottom, and his finger continued to trace a delicate but definitive line along the rounded edge.

"Now this is too good to be true," he murmured excitedly.

Sabrina peered down at him, and for a moment she was taken aback. The obvious intelligence in his gray-green eyes belied the eccentricity she had expected to find, and his wavy brown hair topped a perfectly reasonable face. His features were slightly crooked and wire-rimmed glasses were perched squarely on his aquiline nose, but it was a handsome face, and just now it was filled with anticipation.

"Can I help you?" she asked politely.

"Yes," came the firm reply. He didn't even look up. "I'd appreciate it if you'd be so kind as to get me a ruler."

"A what?"

"A ruler," he repeated. He was so intent on studying something in the limestone that he still hadn't bothered to look up at her. "Oh," he added suddenly, "and a sketch pad if you have one."

Something in his serious manner compelled Sabrina to do his bidding, and with all the courtesy of a good hostess she obliged the man. When she returned in a moment to hand him the requested items, again he failed to look up.

"Perfectly intact," he was saying to himself, taking the ruler and placing it against the statue's bottom. "Just perfect."

Sabrina's curiosity got the better of her. "May I ask what you're doing?" she inquired faintly.

"Just a little investigating," he answered briefly, still engrossed by the stone in front of his nose. "Just a little investigating."

"Oh . . . are you an artist?"

He didn't hear her as he jotted down some numbers on his pad and then went back to measuring. But it was difficult to measure around the curve with the ruler, and he finally tossed it to the floor.

"A tape measure," he said decidedly. "You wouldn't happen to—"

He looked up at last, but stopped in mid-sentence. Sabrina stared down at him candidly, and her gaze was matched by his. His eyes took in her delicate, sensitively molded features, and lingered to gaze into her green eyes. For an instant he seemed to falter. "A tape measure," he repeated dully, but he couldn't seem to stop staring at her. She blinked as he studied her small but sharply delineated chin and her gently pouting mouth.

Sabrina had been told that she had the face of a European model—elegant and refined, with a hint of sensuality just beneath the surface. She wore her glossy chestnut hair pulled into a topknot at the crown of her head, and a long, wavy tail cascaded down from it, curling impishly around one slender shoulder. A gauzy lavender and purple gown covered her petite frame, billowing slightly as she drew an impatient breath.

"What are you measuring?" she asked. Her voice, although still low and distinctly feminine, carried a note of authority as well.

The man tore his eyes away from her face and pointed to the rounded curve of the statue's bottom. "You see these five little bumps?" he asked, pointing to five tiny but distinct protrusions that lined the curve.

"Oh, those," she confirmed, leaning over to look at them. Her artist's vulnerability suddenly shone through as she explained. "I was going to sand those down, but I didn't have time."

"Thank God for small miracles!" he cried.

"What?"

But he was focused once more on the bumps. "That tape measure," he said. "Could you get it for me?"

Sabrina's poise was beginning to vanish. "Look,"

she said, struggling to maintain it, "I'm not a tailor. I'm an artist."

"And I'm a paleontologist," he smiled, shrugging. "Right now I'm amazed at what I'm seeing. You know, I find these things in the craziest places." He laughed, provoking her even more.

"I don't see what's so funny," she fumed. "My work is not supposed to be amusing."

"I'm sorry," he said, waving a hand in dismissal. "It's just that I've been all over the globe on some very far-flown expeditions, but this really takes the cake." He followed an imaginary line along the statue's hip, exclaiming triumphantly when he stopped at another almost-imperceptible protrusion. "Aha! I knew it!"

"Knew what?" she asked doubtfully.

He looked up with a dazzling smile. "Listen, I need a flexible measuring tool of some kind. Are you sure you don't have anything?" She shook her head, and his keen blue eyes darted to the sash around her waist. "How about that belt you're wearing?" he asked, pointing. "Just let me have it for a moment."

She frowned, but then did as he asked. There was something about him she respected, as if he were about to discover a new continent or a new planet.

He took the sash thankfully, then pulled it taut and placed it against the ruler. Taking a pen from the breast pocket of his corduroy jacket, he prepared to mark off the inches.

Sabrina frowned anxiously. "You're going to make marks on my new belt?" she asked.

"Oh! Sorry, I didn't think about that. Well, how about a piece of chalk?"

"Oh, all right." Sabrina sighed resignedly. She elbowed her way through the crowd and picked up the stub of an old drawing pencil from her work table, returning to find him waiting expectantly. Taking the pencil, he began to mark off the protrusions on the statue onto the sash from her dress. Sabrina stood there watching him, wondering whether to leave him to his strange pursuit or to stay and make sure he didn't harm her precious piece of sculpture.

Then he looked up, his expression keenly inquisitive, and asked, "Ontario, right?"

"What about Ontario?" Sabrina found herself becoming bewildered. He had the most provoking habit of jumping randomly from one subject to the next.

"Northern Canada," he explained patiently. "That's where this block of stone came from, right?"

"No." She felt oddly triumphant that he was wrong. "As a matter of fact, I got it in upstate New York."

The stranger shook his head impatiently. "That's impossible."

"But why should I lie to you? I got it from the side of a mountain in the Adirondacks. They were building a highway and I asked the workmen to cut it for me."

He gave the stone a clinical glance. "There's no such rock within a hundred miles of the Adirondacks. What town did you say—"

"I didn't," she broke in sharply. "And I don't see what difference that makes. I certainly wish you'd tell me what this is all about."

"Well, I'm not quite sure yet," he said, his excitement returning. "If I could just get this down . . ." He began to sketch the five protrusions, connecting them with a thin line and adding another on the hip. Sabrina watched over his shoulder as he reproduced them, impressed by his accuracy. His drawing looked like six church bells sitting on a hill.

"Well, I hope you're happy now," she said pragmatically. "And if you don't mind, I'd really appreciate it if you would leave my sculpture alone."

His eyes twinkled. "Oh, don't worry about any

harm being done. As a matter of fact, you're lucky I'm here. I just might make your statue more famous than you ever dreamed."

"It can get famous all by itself," she retorted with justifiable pique. Who was he to come barging in here with his oddball searches and peculiar drawings?

"Of course," he answered politely, but he wasn't really interested. He was still mesmerized by those six little bumps, and Sabrina was suddenly tired of humoring him.

She had waited a very long time to realize her dream of success as an artist, and on Saturday her years of patience would finally be rewarded. She knew without the slightest doubt that *Lady in Flight* was the best piece of work she had ever done. For the last seven years, she had been scraping and struggling in an urban artists' community, continually sacrificing and living on a shoestring in the hope that one day her talent would be recognized. Against the advice of her friends, she had repeatedly refused to sell her early works, preferring instead to hold out until they could command the prices and attention she was sure they deserved.

The invitation to participate in the auction had come as a breathtaking surprise, but even so, she had experienced a secret sense of satisfaction that her stubborn instincts had been correct. The auction had been designed as a benefit by supporters of the National Endowment for the Arts, and would feature promising young artists who had yet to achieve national recognition. Because the artists would split the proceeds with their federal sponsor, potential buyers were afforded the incentive of tax breaks to up their bids. It was anticipated that selling prices would be higher than usual.

Sabrina owed her invitation to participate in the auction not only to the exposure she had garnered from many contests, showings, and contacts she had collected over the years, but to a well-placed acquaintance who had taken an interest in her art *and* helped her support herself until her big break.

It had been necessary, dedication notwithstanding, for Sabrina to provide herself with a means of support during her long climb up the artistic ladder. She had found a way that utilized her creativity even in the face of hard practicality. When she wasn't busy with her painting and sculpture, she designed displays and front windows for department stores on a free-lance basis. There was always enough work to keep her busy, even though she viewed it as a second priority. Her distinctive artistic flair and her delicious sense of the absurd gave her a style that was both unique and appealing, and it was through this odd source of income that she had met her unexpected benefactor.

Arthur Wellington III was the vice-president in charge of marketing at the prestigious department store Lloyd's Fifth Avenue. He had noticed the displays she had done for the store over the summer and had eventually traveled downtown to look at her more serious work. Sabrina knew Mr. Wellington could get her more work in window design. What she hadn't known then was that he was an active member of the board of the National Endowment for the Arts, and thus involved in planning a charity auction featuring young artists.

Wellington had extended the opportunity to be in the auction at the same time that he had asked Sabrina to do Lloyd's fall windows, and she had accepted both offers with alacrity.

Although Sabrina could now dare to hope that her window-dressing days were almost over, the chance to do Lloyd's fall windows was too tempting to turn down. Not only was the pay more than ample, but Lloyd's was famous for its unusual and extravagant windows and she felt that she owed Mr. Wellington something for his generosity.

The idea was to use the Museum of Natural History as a theme. The store would borrow models of pre-historic animals and dinosaur skeletons from the museum, and she would juxtapose them against sleek mannequins dressed in designer fashions and fur coats. The mannequins would be posed walking dinosaurs on leashes or standing in front of caves next to Neanderthal men. The entire concept was whimsical, even outlandish for Sabrina, but she was willing to tackle it. As for Wellington, he was so taken with his idea that he was hiring more people to do over the entire first floor of Lloyd's using the same theme. Sabrina was glad she was responsible for only the windows.

As usual, she was weeks behind schedule on the project, but this did not concern her. She worked best under pressure, and comforted herself with the knowledge that she had at least remembered to send the store a list of the objects she would require from the museum. In the meantime, the upcoming auction was the most important thing in her life. She would let nothing stand in the way of its success.

Sabrina stared down at this strange man who was still examining the bumps on her statue, and realized that he was causing too much of a stir. People had gathered around to watch him, and she didn't want any unfavorable publicity to spread. Whatever he was doing obviously had nothing to do with art. "Well," she said uncertainly, looking down at him, "I guess I'll leave you to your . . . uh . . ." She never finished the sentence, but it didn't matter. He was barely listening, totally absorbed in his work. She backed away unobtrusively, heading in the direction of the kitchen, but her uneasiness changed instantly to delight when she saw who was standing there in the doorway.

"Zeebo!" she cried, waltzing up and throwing her arms around her friend. She spun around lightly, letting her hands swing around his neck. "I'm so glad you could be here!"

Zeebo was munching calmly on a carrot stick, and he bore her enthusiastic greeting with philosophic patience. "I wrote you from Florence that I'd be here," he said, hugging her back. "You know I wouldn't miss this auction for the world." He spoke in the unmistakably self-assured tones of the very rich, but his rather startling appearance gave no indication of wealth.

Dressed in a loose white shirt with a bow tie, wide suspenders, and khaki trousers, he managed to retain an authoritative air despite his youth. His thick, curly hair framed a broad, intelligent face, a face that was as yet unmarked by deep lines of experience.

"It looks like I came just in time," he observed, indicating the crowd around *Lady in Flight.* "Your work is even more popular than I thought it would be."

Sabrina turned and looked at the small gathering of people, stifling a sigh when she realized that it wasn't her sculpture they were admiring, but the stranger and his mysterious examination. He was perched on one knee, and the sash from her dress was looped casually around his neck. Zeebo watched for a moment.

"What is that man doing there?"

"Ruining my chances at the auction," she replied, only half joking. "By the time he's finished, *Lady in Flight* will be renamed *Goosebumps in Flight.*" She told Zeebo all about the bumps on the limestone and the man's keen interest in them. "So you see," she concluded, "he's busy measuring something, and—"

She stopped abruptly, disconcerted by Zeebo's sudden grin. "What are you smiling at?" she demanded. "First him, and now you. This is really too much."

"If Mr. Forrester is doing what I suspect he's doing," Zeebo said, still watching the man's performance, "then your sculpture will be the talk of the town by tomorrow." He began to chuckle quietly, but he stopped when he saw the look on her face.

"I thought it would be the talk of the town anyway," Sabrina protested, ruffled. "Without any help from him. I didn't even invite him, and now he's acting like it's his party."

Zeebo shrugged. "Have it your way."

"I don't even know what he's—" Sabrina stopped again, startled by the connection suddenly forming in her mind. "Did you say Forrester?" she asked after a pause.

"That's right," Zeebo confirmed. "Colin Forrester. He's—"

"From the Museum of Natural History?" Sabrina broke in.

"He's the chief paleontologist there."

"Oh, no!" she groaned, shaking her head in dismay. "Am I in trouble!" After hitting her forehead with her fist, Sabrina ran over to her rolltop desk in the corner of the room. Zeebo followed curiously and watched as she lifted the top to reveal a mountain of unopened mail piled high in the center. He fingered a few of the envelopes, noting the postmarks, some of them more than two weeks old.

"Don't you ever open your mail?" he asked disapprovingly, pulling one airmail letter from the stack. It had been sent from Italy, and the return address bore his name.

"Not for the last two weeks," she admitted. "I've been too busy getting ready for the auction. Anyway, it's bad luck."

"Bad luck?"

"Yes, I never open mail during critical periods in

my life. I can't take the chance that I'll find something to upset or distract me." She was busy riffling
through the envelopes, throwing each one to the side
until she found what she was looking for. "Aha!" She
held the letter up and looked at the return address.
"Colin Forrester, Museum of Natural History."

"Are you sure you want to open it?" Zeebo asked
sardonically. "It won't be bad luck?"

Sabrina shot him a baleful glance. "Very funny."
Her large, expressive eyes stole a peek at the statue to
see if Mr. Forrester was watching her. But he was still
under the *Lady's* spell. She tore open the envelope
and pulled out the letter, scanning it hastily. She
already had a fairly good idea of what it would say,
but she wasn't prepared for Forrester's outrageous
tone. Noting that Sabrina was getting indigant, Zeebo
stood behind her and read over her shoulder.

"Dear Ms. Melendey," it began. "I have just
received a list from Lloyd's Fifth Avenue indicating
which items you would like transferred from the
museum." Sabrina's mouth set in a peevish little
line, as if she knew that there was going to be trouble.
"You can't be serious," the letter continued flatly,
confirming her suspicion. "Do you realize that you
are talking about valuable objects, some of which are
extraordinarily delicate and essential to the
musuem's exhibits? Obviously you have no understanding or appreciation whatsoever of what is
involved here. We cannot possibly move ten models
and arrange ten replacement exhibits at such short
notice. Usually we lend only two or three at a time.
And surely most of them are far too big to fit into any
department store window. I can't imagine what you
could want with all of these items, but it doesn't
really matter, because you aren't going to get them.
We cannot possibly allow you to run willy-nilly
through one of the museum's most popular wings on
practically no notice. You propose to strip my

department almost bare, without regard for the integrity of its structure.

"The people from Lloyd's assured me this project would be handled in a responsible, professional manner. If your list is any indication of the kind of professionalism you have in mind, then we are off to a very poor start indeed."

Sabrina was already frowning darkly, an angry flush spreading over her smooth countenance, but the last sentence of the letter almost made her explode.

"Perhaps, if you cannot handle this responsibility, it would be best if we found someone else, someone more reliable, in whom I can place my trust." The letter was signed, "Sincerely yours, Colin Forrester."

"That smug meathead!" Sabrina exclaimed furiously. "How dare he use that condescending, insulting tone?"

Zeebo's attention was diverted, however, by the sudden hum of conversation that emanated from the other side of the room. The crowd around *Lady in Flight* was buzzing with anticipation, as if the strange man were about to reveal something.

"Come on," Zeebo said, taking her arm and leading her through the crowd. "I think you'd better investigate."

Sabrina held her temper in check and walked back to Colin Forrester, who was smiling broadly, the sketch pad in his hand. "Are you finished there?" she asked levelly.

"Not quite," he responded, beaming like a schoolboy who had just gotten a gold star. "Come and have a look."

Impulsively, he pulled her down next to him on the floor. The surrounding group was quiet, waiting for him to explain what it was he had been investigating.

"You see these?" he asked, pointing meticulously

to the five protrusions. "And this?" he added, touching the statue's hip. He then drew an imaginary but distinct line down the statue's leg. "And all the way down to here." He looked at her proudly, and she met his glance with one of total perplexity. "Seymouria," he concluded grandly. "At least that's what I think it is." He looked around at the group as if expecting a round of applause, but none was forthcoming. Zeebo grinned, but Sabrina maintained a blank stare. "I won't know for sure until I scrape away at this section here—"

At this Sabrina reacted, her expression giving way to cold disbelief. "You're a nut!" she proclaimed decidedly.

"Not at all," he countered calmly. "Take a look at this." He produced the sketch pad and pointed to a drawing that depicted a series of bones.

"It's—it's a skeleton!" Sabrina gasped.

And so it was. The drawing now took shape, and the church bells on the hill became the joints of some peculiar animal that vaguely resembled an alligator.

"Seymouria," he said again, nodding sagely. "Of course I could be wrong, but I have a hunch that that's what it is."

"Are you telling me," Sabrina said slowly, "that there's a—a dead animal in my sculpture?"

"A fossilized animal," he corrected. "And it's only the skeleton."

"Oh," she said faintly.

He pointed clinically to the protrusions. "These are part of the backbone. What I want to know now is whether the entire animal is intact, or if only this one piece remains." His eyes shone with enthusiasm, as if he were looking at a long-lost Picasso.

"But—but that shouldn't make any difference," she fluttered, her gown billowing gently around her ankles. "You don't seem to understand. This is a work of art, not a—a specimen of some kind."

But he wasn't listening. He was examining the fossil again, flicking at one of the tiny bumps with a carefully controlled finger. "Well, what do you know," he murmured.

"What?" Sabrina asked in alarm. "What is it?" She bent over to look again, and the crowd all leaned forward to look too.

"It might not be a seymouria after all," he mused, impressed. "In fact, it could even be . . ." Before she could stop him, Forrester whipped out a small penknife and began to methodically scrape at one of the miniscule bumps.

"What do you think you're doing?" Sabrina demanded, horrified. She reached over hastily and pushed his hand away.

He was unperturbed. "I'm just doing a little scientific exploration," he answered mildly.

"Not on my sculpture, you're not!" Her astonished gaze traveled beseechingly to the onlookers, who appeared just as shocked as she felt.

But he remained bent on exploring his find. His hand moved back to the protrusions, but Sabrina grabbed it and held it fast. "Stop that!" she commanded. His fingers wrapped around hers and he smiled.

"Do you realize this thing is over three hundred and fifty million years old?" he asked, the excitement returning to color his voice.

Sabrina stared at him in confusion. Was he serious? He certainly seemed to be, and yet there was the glimmer of a teasing smile around the corners of his clear, gray-green eyes. The glimmer deepened as he let her hand go, and he pointed at the statue's bottom.

"I'm very impressed," he said judgmentally. "I wouldn't be surprised if this fellow's tail goes right down your lady's left leg. And if my estimations are correct, his head lies somewhere about . . ." He slowly traced a line around the statue's hip and continued upward, stopping at the right breast. "Here!" he finished triumphantly, patting the breast for emphasis.

Sabrina frowned, and a few of the guests giggled. "I suspect this could be an early amphibian," he concluded, addressing his audience with confidence. "Probably a seymouria, or perhaps a later relative."

"I'm not interested in Seymour's relatives," Sabrina joked in an attempt to squelch all further interest. "This whole thing is ridiculous. So what if some reptile left his footprints in that stone? Whatever he was doing there has been over for a long time. He is no longer welcome!"

"But don't you think it's unusual for a fossil to remain completely intact inside a piece of sculpture?" he persisted. He hunched down again to admire the bumps, and looked up at Sabrina with a quizzical air. The onlookers began to disperse, tired of his antics, and Sabrina breathed a private sigh of relief. Someone put a record on the stereo, and cool, syncopated jazz rhythms bounced appealingly through the large room.

Sabrina was tempted to leave him squatting there. She didn't want to draw any more attention to him. Things were bad enough already. Catching a piece of conversation from a nearby group, she surmised that the five protrusions—no, make that six—were now common knowledge. The last thing she needed was for his discovery to eclipse her art.

"I really should have filed those silly bumps down," she muttered in spite of herself. "Now everyone knows about them, and they'll probably talk about that and nothing else. Do you realize what you've done?" she asked Forrester accusingly.

His keen eyes narrowed slightly, but he smiled again. "Why, yes. I've just made a most observant discovery. You should be glad."

"*Glad?*" She almost choked. "Why should I be

glad?" She stepped back as he stood up suddenly, and was surprised, now that they were standing side by side, to see how tall he was. She expected his answer to be condescending, but he was too genuinely delighted with his find to put on airs.

"Well, it's rather an honor, don't you think?" he asked almost humbly.

A crackpot, Sabrina said to herself. A hopeless academic with his nose glued to a textbook and no concern for anything else, especially art. She stifled a sigh. "No, I don't think it's an honor. I think it's a nuisance. Your little discovery may drive the value of my work down. People may not be so eager to buy a piece of sculpture with that—that creature in it."

He laughed boyishly and nodded several times. "True. But that won't really be a problem." He dug in his pocket and, to her surprise, pulled out a checkbook. "How much do you want for it?"

Sabrina flushed with anger. "You want to buy it? Just like that? Why? So you can tear it apart and resurrect that stupid reptile?"

"It's not a reptile," he said patiently. "It's an early amphibian."

"Oh." She didn't know whether to argue or to ignore him, when suddenly she remembered the letter and envelope she still held in her hand. Her guilty glance at them betrayed her thoughts, and he followed her gaze with a knowing expression.

"Don't tell me that's the letter I wrote you," he said, clearly annoyed. "Don't you believe in opening your mail?"

"I just did," she informed him. "What a charming letter it was. You don't exactly know how to win friends and influence people, do you, Mr. Forrester?"

He didn't flinch. "I tried to call you several times. If you had answered my calls, I wouldn't have written that letter."

"I was too busy," she said, vaguely waving an arm.

"I had to finish *Lady in Flight* in time for tomorrow. I couldn't be bothered with all this dinosaur business." She sighed impatiently. "Besides, I'm not scheduled to get started on those windows until next month. Why are you in such a rush?"

Completely exasperated with her attitude, the academic ran a hand through his light brown hair. "This is next month," he pointed out. "Starting tomorrow."

"Is it?" she replied, a little startled. "Then you'll have to wait until then for an answer." Without giving him a chance to reply, Sabrina sailed past him and floated back into the party.

What a pest, she thought irritably. What a bona fide screwball. She turned to glance quickly at him and saw that he still stood in the same spot, glaring at her. Sabrina tried to stare him down, but it was no use. Feeling oddly ill at ease, she marched into the kitchen. Maybe he'll just leave quietly, she thought hopefully. Then I'll be rid of him.

Chapter Two

Colin watched as Sabrina disappeared into the haze and smoke, an angry expression on his face. Who did she think she was? Bent on following her, he was so intent on evening the score that he ran smack into Zeebo, who was walking forward with a drink in his hand. The contents of his glass splashed them both, and Colin immediately stepped back.

"Oh, I'm so sorry," he offered. "I didn't see you coming."

Zeebo smiled tolerantly. "No harm done." He took a sip from his glass and measured Colin with his eyes. "You were quite excited by *Lady in Flight* a moment ago, weren't you?"

"*Lady in Flight*? Oh, you mean the . . ." Colin jerked his head back in the direction of the statue. "Right. That's a very remarkable piece of limestone."

"It's more than that," Zeebo countered. "It's Sabrina's greatest triumph. It took her six months to create, and I should know. I watched her start it, I watched her throw out dozens of preliminary sketches, and I continued to watch as she made it into a reality."

"I see," Colin answered quietly, finally subduing his scientific bent. "It really is very good. Of course I'm no great judge, but—"

"You don't have to be," Zeebo broke in decisively. "Anyone can see it's a masterpiece." He stared at the statue for a moment, and his face betrayed his genuine appreciation. "I'd give anything to buy it."

"Then why don't you?" Colin asked affably.

"Because," Zeebo smiled ruefully. "Sabrina won't let me. I've been trying to buy her paintings for years." He gestured grandly to the far side of the loft, where a large number of canvases were lodged against the wall.

"You see all those?" he asked. Colin nodded, fascinated in spite of himself. "She refused to sell even one."

"But why?" Colin pressed, amazed.

"Because she's stubborn. I think she's too stubborn, but that's just how she is." He shrugged philosophically.

"I don't understand. If she doesn't want to sell her work, then why is she participating in the auction tomorrow?

Zeebo toyed with the corner of his bow tie, looking at Colin with frank interest. "You know, Mr. Forrester, you're reputed to be a brilliant man. But I can see you don't know much about art."

"I guess not," Colin admitted. He never minded admitting when he didn't know something; after all, he could always learn.

"Sabrina's been struggling for years," Zeebo explained. "A lot of the artists around here struggle for years, but they never make it. Sabrina has been holding out, waiting until she had the one truly great piece that would command a lot of attention. She always knew that once she could make it with that one piece, all of her other work would be worth just as much. She's waited a long time, and she's about to see her dream come true."

"But I still don't understand," Colin frowned. "If you were willing to buy her paintings at a good price . . ."

"I was. But she wouldn't sell them to me." Zeebo

sighed. "She was afraid I wasn't totally objective, that I was only patronizing her. She wanted to be absolutely sure that she made it on her own."

"I see. So she's an undiscovered genius living in the proverbial garret and waiting for the big break?"

"Something like that." Zeebo smiled, but carefully, his loyalty to Sabrina evident.

Colin watched him curiously, and couldn't resist asking, "You're not . . . ?" He indicated Sabrina delicately, and Zeebo got the message, amusement and a little consternation overtaking his broad face.

"Me? Oh, no, absolutely not. I'm too young for her, for one thing. And—well, I just don't think she's ever thought of me that way." Zeebo hid his face in his glass for a moment, and Colin was amused. At last the self-assured young man had revealed some vulnerability.

"So you're just very good friends," he concluded evenly.

"That's right."

"And are you an artist too?"

Again Zeebo seemed amused. "Who, me? Good heavens, no."

"But you certainly seem to know a lot about what goes on in the art world," Colin persisted.

"That's true. But I hang around here because I enjoy it and because I can afford to."

"Oh. Are you rich?"

Zeebo nodded. "Yes," he replied matter-of-factly. "I'm independently wealthy. Loaded, to be exact." He looked down, indicating his odd clothing. "All this is just an affectation."

Colin was too surprised to answer, so he tried to smile pleasantly. "Well," he sputtered finally, "at least you're honest about it."

"Honest? Oh, yes, I can afford to be. But that's why I like Sabrina so much. She's the most honest person I know, and she's a free spirit. Excuse me. I have to go and say hello to that woman over there. I don't know why Sabrina bothers to invite her. She's only interested in art that matches her carpeting." He sprinted off, leaving a bemused Colin to fend for himself.

Caught in the swirl of people, Colin wended his way over to the bar and poured himself a drink. He stood alone for a moment, surveying the startling blend of people, and decided to try to talk to Sabrina again. Perhaps he had been too hasty with her. After all, it was obvious that she only decorated store windows as a means of income while she pursued her true vocation. He smiled to himself, tried to tap his foot in time to the jazz recording, and discovered he couldn't.

"So, you're that famous anthropologist." The voice was booming and Brooklyn-accented, and it came from behind.

Colin turned and saw a short, stocky man wearing a plaid flannel shirt. "Paleontologist," he corrected with a smile. "I'm into bones."

"Yeah, dinosaurs, right?" The man extended a large hand. "I'm Sal Mattucci, Sabrina's postman." His handshake was warm and hearty. "I saw you looking at the statue over there, and I kinda wondered what you were doing. I thought you had some sorta perversion or something, until I heard you say there's a dinosaur hidden in there."

"Uh—yes." Colin was a little embarrassed. He went on rapidly to explain about the fossil and how it might be valuable, and Sal nodded enthusiastically, punctuating the narrative frequently with, "Uh-huh." As Colin continued, he had the uneasy feeling that Sal didn't understand a word he was saying, but he noticed a neatly dressed Japanese man standing next to them who was listening with obvious interest. The man waited patiently for a break in the conversation, and then stepped forward.

"Mishiro Ibisito Tashomi," he said, extending a

hand. "Call me Mishi." Colin shook his hand obligingly and started to say something, but Sal stepped forward eagerly and pumped the newcomer's hand also. Mishi accepted the greeting politely, but turned his attention back to Colin.

"You and I have a great deal in common," he said earnestly. "I have dedicated my life to dinosaurs."

"Oh." Colin's face lit up. He was happy to have found an ally in this crowd of art lovers. "You're a scientist?"

"No, I'm a filmmaker."

Colin was puzzled. "I don't understand. I thought—"

"I make monster movies," Mishi explained hastily. "My last picture was *Godzilla Meets the Space Monster*. Maybe you saw it. It was a big hit back in Japan."

"I'm sure Mr. Forrester doesn't go to those kinds of movies, Mishi." It was Sabrina, floating up next to the filmmaker as if prepared to protect him. The look on her face was pleasant but challenging. Colin gave her a neutral smile, which she returned at once. "He's probably too busy poring over his old paleontology journals," she continued smoothly. "Isn't that right, Mr. Forrester?"

His eyebrow lifted archly. "As a matter of fact, Ms. Melendey, you couldn't be more—"

"Hey!" Sal broke in, addressing Mishi excitedly. "Did you say *Godzilla Meets the Space Monster*? I saw that one! The one where the big tyrannosaurus destroys Tokyo?"

"No." Mishi's smile was a bit pained. Colin blinked, and Sabrina looked distinctly amused. "You're thinking of *Godzilla*, the original. In my picture, the monster destroys Cleveland."

Sal nodded, contrite.

"What makes you think I'm such a stick-in-the-mud?" Colin said directly to Sabrina, still piqued by her remark. "Let the man ask his question. I might just surprise you."

"You see," Mishi began seriously, "I've been making monster movies for years—"

But again Sal interrupted, his enthusiasm boundless. "*King Kong Meets Godzilla!*" He pointed a finger at the filmmaker. "Right? Am I right?"

Mishi nodded modestly, still trying to get back to Colin.

"Now I know who you are," Sal beamed. "I've seen them all." He went down the list of monster movies he had relished, much to Colin's amusement and Mishi's surprise. Sabrina watched him with something very much like affection. "The one where Gonga destroys New York, the one where Son of Gonga swallows the Pacific Ocean, and, uh . . . uh . . ." He looked questioningly at the filmmaker, who waited curiously. "Uh . . . uh, now don't tell me—" He tapped his head a few times, trying to jolt his memory. "Oh, yeah, I remember, the one with the triceratops that demolishes Mount Everest—"

"*Torgo the Terrible!*" Colin exclaimed suddenly. The other three looked at him, utterly surprised. There was a small silence, during which Sabrina's amazement was plainly evident, and Colin gave her a cool, deliberate glance. "I like to watch the late movies," he explained to his still-enthralled audience.

Mishi was encouraged. "Have you seen any of my other films?" he asked hopefully.

"No, I don't think so. *Torgo* was the only one."

"Well, Mr. Forrester," Mishi continued, "I wanted to ask you—that is, if you don't mind—well, if you think my monsters are accurately portrayed. I mean to say, are they realistic? Are they to scale?"

Colin drew a deep breath, stealing a look at Sabrina. Her eyes seemed to be challenging him once again. "Actually, Mishi," he said carefully, "I don't think it really matters. There never were any three-hundred-

foot-high monsters—uh, I mean dinosaurs." He
found himself going into something of an explanation, during which Sal lost interest, and Mishi
nodded intently several times. Sabrina looked mildly
dissatisfied, but said nothing. At length Sal backed
away, heading for a refill of his drink, and Mishi
smiled politely.

"Perhaps I will scale my monsters down to size,"
he mused. "Perhaps a tyrannosaurus—"

Colin shook his head. "Not if you want realism.
There never was a tyrannosaurus that could have
destroyed a whole city. But I doubt your audience
minds. They're just looking for a good adventure."
Mishi thanked him and moved off.

"Did you have to be so scientific?" Sabrina asked
the moment the filmmaker was out of earshot. She
was pouting slightly, silently accusing him of being a
killjoy. "Mishiro is very serious about his work, you
know," she added.

"I know that. And that's why I told him the truth.
He asked me, you know."

"Are you always so literal?" she frowned.

"Sometimes," he countered. "But not when I'm
watching the late show."

Sabrina smiled slowly, her eyes assessing him. But
all she said was, "I have to go and check on the food.
Will you excuse me?"

"Oh, I'm always interested in food," he said
quickly. "I'll help you." He followed her through the
crowd into the kitchen, which was surprisingly
equipped with all kinds of sophisticated cookware.
The rest of the loft was airy and light, mostly because
there was hardly any furniture, but the kitchen
reflected the obvious dedication of a skilled cook.
Sabrina had not objected to his offer of help, and he
suspected she might be ready to talk reasonably.

"Enjoying yourself, Mr. Forrester?" she asked.

"Colin," he said. "And yes, I am. I may not be an

expert on modern art, but when it comes to good food, I have unlimited enthusiasm." His eyes darted appreciatively around the kitchen, noting the many covered bowls and platters. Lifting the aluminum foil from one of the bowls, he dipped a finger tentatively inside and took a taste. "Mmmm," he said, impressed. "What is this? It's delicious."

"Macaroni salad, Mr. Forrester," she answered airly. "Just plain old macaroni salad."

The unspoken truce they had established seemed suddenly very fragile, and he decided to take a commanding stance. "Now look," he said, "you're not going to let what's happened tonight obstruct our relationship, are you?"

"What relationship?" Sabrina retorted. "All I know is that you've got a museum full of dinosaurs that I need, and I've got a mummified creature entombed in my sculpture."

"Not mummified," he amended patiently. "Fossilized." He smiled thinly. "And I'm only doing my job."

"Famous last words! Can't you think about anything except your great pursuit of old bones?"

"That reminds me," he rejoined promptly. "I'd like to get a look at that thing again before I leave."

Sabrina let out a sound of pure frustration. "You really don't know when to stop, do you? I've got news for you, Einstein. My lack of responsibility, as you call it, seems matched only by your gross insensitivity." She began to remove covers and lids, banging them down on counters, and looking for serving spoons. "Lloyd's hired me to do their windows, and I intend to do them."

He folded his arms across his chest defiantly. "But first you'll have to have clearance from me. And you have to admit, your requests are perfectly outrageous."

Her eyes narrowed. "Are you aware," she said

slowly, realizing she had a line of attack she thought he couldn't dispute, "that the store has made a very generous gift to the musuem in the form of a research grant for over half a million dollars? I think they're entitled to a little cooperation, don't you?"

Much to her obvious annoyance, Colin reacted to her grand speech by laughing self-confidently. "Cooperation is one thing, but asking me to snap my fingers and at the drop of a hat produce all those models—some of which you don't even seem to be sure you'll use—and leave them standing in the midst of ladies' lingerie next to mannequins in fur coats is outlandish, to say the least."

She closed her eyes for a moment, as if trying to summon the patience he lacked. "That, my dear Mr. Forrester, is the whole point. It's *supposed* to be outlandish. And you're supposed to cooperate."

He blinked and for a moment could think of nothing to say. She noted this calmly, and added, "Don't forget the caveman with the spear. I want him standing right next to a mannequin dressed in pelts. Quite a statement, don't you think?"

"Very amusing," he said frostily. "But I can't see that there's any point to it."

"Is that so?" she shouted, losing her temper completely. "You think you know all about everything, don't you? Well, we'll just see what your boss has to say about that."

"I *am* the boss," he shouted back, gleefully triumphant. "And we don't need half a million dollars thrown in our faces when you're talking about threatening the integrity of the museum's reputation. Why, the museum is a highly respected institution! You have no idea what it means to scholarship, to the city, even to you!"

It was her turn to be speechless. She stared at him coldly, but he could sense her loss of composure.

"Money can't buy everything," he finished in a judicious tone.

Sabrina found her voice. "Then why—"

"Publicity," he broke in with measured simplicity. "We thought we could use the exposure." He did nothing to eliminate the rather smug expression from his face, and she turned away, loading bowls onto a large tray. He watched her for a moment, leaning over to sample a deliciously lumpy-looking chocolate-covered peanut. "Nice and crunchy," he pronounced. "Roasted peanuts?"

She glanced over and smiled. "No, Mr. Forrester. Those are chocolate-covered grasshoppers." Shouldering through the swinging door, she exited breezily from the kitchen.

Colin choked and then gamely swallowed. He was about to leave the kitchen when the door swung open again, hitting him squarely in the side. Sabrina entered, her hands free, and she met his sour look with a dazzling smile. She went over to the oven, reaching for a pot holder, but when she tried to open the oven door, she found that it was stuck fast. He watched, amazed, as she matter-of-factly picked up a can opener and hit the oven door on its hinges. It popped open immediately, and she calmly reached inside to retrieve a tray of rolls. Colin burst out laughing, his anger and outrage suddenly diminished.

"Am I that amusing?" Sabrina asked.

"You do have unique methods," he observed.

There was a small silence between them. An unspoken truce was bobbing near the surface, but Colin couldn't find a safely neutral topic. Sabrina, however, could.

"Would you mind getting the ice out of the freezer?" she asked, her tone friendly.

Amenable to her cordiality, he peered inside the refrigerator, and was somehow reassured to find that it was filled to overflowing with food. At least this provoking little waif didn't starve herself for art.

As he reached for the ice, she noticed a long, fresh scar on the side of his hand. She pointed and bluntly asked, "What's that?"

"This?" He grinned and held his hand up to the light, affording her a closer view. "I was bitten by a tyrannosaurus rex." His eyes sparkled mischievously, and she met his smile with a look of severe disbelief. "It's true," he insisted, breaking into laughter. "You see, I was on an expedition in Mongolia, and there was this really exciting fossil on the other side of the cliff in the—"

He was interrupted by two very vivacious young women who swung through the door impatiently. The first was tall and sleek, with very straight black hair, and the second was shorter and rounder, with an untamed mane of dark curls. "Need any help?" they chimed.

"Veronica! Allegra! It's great to see you!" Sabrina sailed past him and threw her arms around her two friends. The three laughed together in the small kitchen and exchanged greetings, until Veronica peered over Sabrina's shoulder to examine the tall, lanky man who stood quietly watching them.

"How do you do?" she asked coolly. "I'm Veronica Coyne."

"And I'm Allegra Russo," added her shorter friend.

Sabrina continued the introductions. "These are two of my closest friends," she told Colin. "When we were in college, we started a group called the Mangia Society. Today it's a regular organization with hundreds of members, and Allegra is the president." She nodded toward Allegra, and the young woman nodded pleasantly.

"What's the Mangia Society?" Colin asked.

"It's a club dedicated to the celebration of enjoyment of great food," Allegra answered. She and

Veronica were both looking at him with undisguised curiosity. Sabrina laughed and turned to Colin.

"This is Colin Forrester," she announced. "The famous proctologist."

"Paleontologist!" he fumed.

"Not the way I see it," she persisted. "Anyone who squats down to study my statue's—"

"Oh, boy," Veronica broke in, shaking her head, "let me know if I should duck all the flying sparks."

Allegra laughed and began to organize the disarray in the kitchen. Colin watched in awe as she deftly unmolded a cold fish mousse onto a round platter and then turned to a container of mushrooms, slicing them with dazzling speed. He was feeling distinctly uncomfortable in the midst of this sudden show of feminine solidarity, and he was in no mood for gameplaying. He cast a meaningful look at Sabrina, saying, "I'll catch you later," before heading through the swinging door.

Allegra shot Sabrina a coy, knowing smile. "Who was that?" she asked with no small interest.

"Oh . . . just some scientist who's giving me a hard time," Sabrina answered irritably.

Veronica's eyes twinkled. "I think he's cute," she teased.

"He is not," Sabrina snapped, causing Colin, who'd been listening through the door, to jerk up his head in surprise at her vehemence. He knew he was eavesdropping and decided he didn't want to hear more, especially after a muffled comment of Allegra's was answered by both Veronica and Sabrina's giggles. He moved away.

The smoke and conversation of the party swirled around him. What he really wanted was to go and have another look at that fossil, but he didn't want to cause a scene. He ambled over to one corner and stood by the door, watching the lively crowd for a moment. A sudden knock on the door startled him, and, surmising that the hostess was still busy in the kitchen, he stepped over and opened it. A stocky, middle-aged man stood at the threshold, dressed in well-worn working clothes and holding a large and greasy brown paper parcel. He smiled at Colin and said, "Cheese. I brought up a whole assortment."

"Oh! I see. Here, let me . . ." Colin dug into his pocket and pulled out a dollar tip. "Here," he said congenially. "For your trouble." The man took it but looked rather confused. Then he smiled, as if very amused at something, and handed the parcel to Colin. Sabrina came out of the kitchen and came over immediately, taking the parcel from Colin's outstretched arms. "Delivery man just brought this," he said.

Sabrina did a slight double take, then sighed elaborately as she made introductions. "Colin Forrester," she said, "I'd like you to meet Arthur Wellington III. Mr. Wellington is the vice-president in charge of merchandising at Lloyd's Fifth Avenue," she added pointedly. "And it's because of his attention that my work is going to be auctioned."

Colin was immediately contrite. "Oh, I'm sorry, Mr. Wellington. I had no idea. I thought you were—"

"Yes, I could see what you thought," the man chuckled, as he pocketed the money with a what-the-heck grin. "I must say, it was a surprise." He looked down ruefully at his clothes. "I didn't have time to change. I was out playing baseball with my son's team."

"That's quite all right," Sabrina assured him hastily. "And it was so nice of you to bring the cheese assortment." She shot Colin a glance that looked very much like a warning.

"Forrester . . . Forrester," Wellington mused. "Ah! The paleontologist?"

"That's right," Colin answered.

"Oh, of course," Wellington affirmed. "From the

museum. We're certainly looking forward to those windows. I understand you'll be helping Sabrina out with them. She's very creative, isn't she?"

"Thank you, Arthur," Sabrina said graciously, taking his arm and squeezing it fondly. She threw Colin another glance, as if to suggest that he might say something horribly embarrassing or inappropriate, and he met the look with one of apologetic innocence.

"I read about that expedition of yours last year," the vice-president was saying. "Was it true you were bitten by a tyrannosaurus rex?"

Colin looked straight at Sabrina and smiled triumphantly. Then he held up his hand to reveal the scar. "Scout's honor," he said. "Of course, it was dead at the time, but those old bones are still pretty sharp."

"That's very interesting." Wellington's tone was sincere. "And what's your next adventure going to be?"

"Oh, I don't know. I might go forage for fossils at the Museum of Modern Art."

Sabrina blanched, groping desperately for a change of subject. But Wellington provided it for her.

"Excuse me," he said. "I've got to go and have another look at that statue of yours. This is Sabrina's first auction, and I want the chance to bid, just like everyone else." He glided away, leaving a very provoked Sabrina to deal with Colin. She turned to face him directly, the degree of her frustration apparent on her face.

"Okay, okay," he said immediately, backing off. "I'll make a deal with you."

"What kind of deal?" she asked suspiciously.

"I'll stop drawing attention to that fossil if you'll agree to let me come back and look at it later." He tried to sound businesslike, but he couldn't help the scientifically motivated zeal that crept into his voice.

"I just want to take some measurements," he added. "I won't scrape at anything."

She considered. "Does that mean you'll leave right now?" she asked hopefully.

"I will if I can get another look at that statue before the auction. Besides, I'll have to get some measuring tools."

"It's a deal," Sabrina said, taking his arm and leading him over to the door.

"I'll be back," he said with a prophetic air as he stepped out.

Sabrina breathed a sigh of relief and went back to her party, pausing in spite of herself to look at *Lady in Flight*. It was a slender, fluid work, seemingly in motion, and she couldn't help being proud of it. But as her gaze traveled down, her eyes stopped at the five protrusions. Now that they had drawn so much attention, they were all she could see. It was like having heard one wrong note in a symphony or one missed line in a play. The mistake loomed above the harmony in her memory and bothered her.

As the evening wore on, she circled and chatted with her friends and with the people who had become interested in the auction. All of them hoped to cash in on a good find, and her excitement mounted as she accepted the compliments of people she had long wanted to impress. At last the guests began to dwindle, and the loft slowly emptied itself, leaving only Sabrina, Zeebo, Veronica, and Allegra. Her old friends pitched in cheerfully, helping to clear the place up. Zeebo collected the empty glasses and plates, Veronica stationed herself at the sink, and Allegra transferred all of the remaining food into containers.

A few minutes after midnight, Zeebo straightened his bow tie and announced, "Well, darling, that's it for me. I'm heading out."

"So soon?" Sabrina's voice was teasing. "You never go to bed before three in the morning."

He called her bluff. "Who said anything about bed?" he drawled. "I'm going over to the Village to meet the new jazz pianist everyone's talking about. We're going out for a late snack at the Empire Diner. Care to join us?"

Sabrina stifled a yawn and shook her head. "No thanks. But have a good time."

"Oh, I will. Good night." He kissed her on the cheek and left.

"It was a great party," Veronica said, coming out of the kitchen.

"Great food," Allegra added with a wry smile—she'd provided much of the food. "You look exhausted, Sabrina. Why don't you go and take a nice, relaxing bath and climb into bed? We'll finish up here."

Sabrina smiled gratefully. "I'll take you up on that. Thanks for your contributions, Allegra. As usual, you outdid yourself." She gave each of them a hug and then went into the bathroom to fill the tub with sudsy water. Ten minutes later, she stepped luxuriously into the hot water and let herself sink deliciously into the frothy bubbles. The hot, soothing water rippled pleasantly over her limbs, and she relaxed, too tired to do anything but lie there for a while, her slender frame hidden by the clouds of foam. Only her knees and the pale pinks tips of her breasts poked through the bubbles occasionally, as the water swelled and then ebbed in barely perceptible motion.

Sabrina closed her eyes, allowing the seductive warmth to claim her. She inhaled deeply, smelling the scent of jasmine bath oil. When her eyes fluttered open, she saw that the bubbles had remained firm. The sounds of activity could still be heard from the outer room, and she surmised that her friends were still cleaning up. Nice of them . . .

A loud bang made her sit up suddenly, trails of bubbles slithering down her arms. She looked up in alarm. It was the bathroom door! Who had slammed it? If it was shut too hard, it would stick.

Climbing hastily out of the tub, Sabrina ran over and tried the door. As she had feared, it was jammed solidly.

"Hey!" she called frantically. "Veronica? Allegra? Is that you?"

She could hear footsteps coming toward the door, followed by a polite knock.

"Hello, Sabrina," came a now-familiar voice. "I'm back."

Chapter Three

❧

"Help!" she exclaimed. "I'm locked in here!"

The doorknob rattled. "Sabrina?" Colin called. "Are you through in the bath?"

"Who cares if I'm through! Get me out of here!"

The doorknob rattled again several times, but nothing happened. This was followed by a few swift kicks, but the door remained stuck.

"How did you manage to trap yourself in there?" he asked impatiently, still shaking the doorknob.

"It wasn't my fault," she answered weakly. "This door sticks if it's closed too quickly."

"Oh. It figures," he muttered, and added. "I, er, closed it because I thought you were in there and didn't want to embarrass you. But, um, don't worry, I'll get you out."

Sabrina stood naked and dripping with suds, listening anxiously as he continued to fight with the recalcitrant lock, swearing under his breath at his continued failure.

"Try a hammer and wedge," she called after a small, ominous silence. "In the kitchen, first drawer on the left."

He said something incomprehensible and stalked off into the kitchen, where she could hear him rummaging through the drawer. As his footsteps approached once more, she reached hastily for her towel—but it wasn't there. She looked around frantically and remembered, too late, that she had left it draped over the chair outside.

There was nowhere to go but back into the tub. She retreated speedily, stepping back into the warm water and trying as best as she could to cover herself with the dwindling bubbles.

The door shook menacingly as he applied the tools, and Sabrina cowered in the tub. Then, after one well-placed blow, it sprang open and Colin flew unceremoniously into the room. He looked down at her, half-covered by bubbles, and began to laugh.

Sabrina opened her mouth to say something but closed it again immediately. As annoyed as she was, she was in no position to argue.

She had expected him to react, of course. She had thought he might be surprised, hopefully even embarrassed. Even out-and-out masculine interest would have been understandable under the circumstances. But laughter?

"Would you mind handing me my towel?" she asked frostily. "It's hanging over the chair just outside the door."

Still chuckling merrily, he strolled out and returned a moment later, the towel draped over one arm. Without thinking, he reached out casually and gave the door a shove. It slammed shut with a decisive bang, and he looked at Sabrina with dismay.

"Oh, no," he groaned, his laughter cut short.

She said nothing; she didn't have to. The look on her face said it all as he went back to the door.

"Maybe we'll get lucky," he suggested hopefully as he tried to open it. They didn't. Sure enough, the door was stuck once again.

"Oh, Lord," he said, rattling the knob. "Not again."

"This time it's definitely your fault," she said sternly, squirming beneath her scanty covering.

"*My* fault? Don't you ever bother to fix things around here?" He was wrestling furiously with the knob, but it wouldn't budge. "How can you live like this?"

"That's my business," she answered loftily.

"Well." He gave up the struggle and turned to face her. This time he didn't laugh, and his gaze traveled frankly down the length of her slender form. "What's the technique for getting out of here from the inside?"

Her face fell. "There isn't one."

"Oh." He drew a deep breath. "All right . . ."

Sabrina wished he would stop looking at her that way. He was wearing his clinical look, but this time it wasn't directed at a piece of stone. It was aimed directly at her.

"Uh . . . would you mind handing me that towel?"

"Towel? Oh, of course! Here." He handed it to her with a grin. She took it and held it over the edge of the tub, but he didn't move. He just continued to stand there looking at her with a wicked grin.

The truth was that Colin couldn't really see all that much of her, but she looked so elusively appealing that he couldn't resist feasting his eyes. When his gaze returned to her face—that extraordinary, piquant face—he caught the beseeching look in her eyes and was aware of her discomfort.

"I'll . . . have another try at that door," he murmured. The minute his back turned, Sabrina sprang up and wrapped herself gratefully in the towel, tucking the ends in as tightly as she could.

She watched anxiously as Colin fought another round with the door, his frustration growing as he continued to struggle. "Of all the damn—" He maintained a one-sided dialogue with the door that was peppered with various threatening oaths, but the door was unconvinced.

"Why don't you try using the hammer?" she suggested.

"Because the hinges are on the outside. It won't

make any—oh, what the heck. Here, hold this." He handed her the wedge and she took it. As she did, the towel began to slip alarmingly, and she grabbed it hastily, tucking the ends back in.

The hammer succeeded only in making a large dent in the brass doorknob. Sabrina rolled her eyes and said impatiently, "Let me do that."

He raised an eyebrow and couldn't help looking at the top of the towel, which was slipping down to reveal the swell of her breasts. She pulled it up and reached for the hammer at the same time, but the hammer escaped her grasp and fell to the floor, hitting her squarely on the toe.

"Ow!" she yelled, hopping up and down on one foot. She continued to dance around the bathroom floor, the towel held up by one hand and her foot by the other. "Ow, ow ow!" She soothed her throbbing toe and looked accusingly at Colin.

"Sorry," he said mildly, bending down to pick up the hammer.

"Oh, give me that!" She pulled the hammer from his hand and reached for the wedge, but the towel was once again sliding down her slender body. Holding it against her breasts with one hand, she angled the wedge into the seam between the door and the wall. Then she aimed the hammer and gave it a good hard bang.

A chip of wood flew into the air. Colin caught it neatly and exclaimed, "You are a good chiseler!"

Sabrina only cast him a glance and hit the wedge again. "Now I know why you were bitten by a dinosaur," she said self-righteously. "You're very careless."

"I'm careless!" he flared. "That's a laugh! Anyone who can live like this—"

Sabrina stopped and held the hammer threateningly above his head. "One more word and I'll hit you on the head with both hands."

He brightened immediately. "Ah, then maybe the towel will fall off altogether."

Sabrina clutched the towel to her body. "It's really very rude of you to point that out. You shouldn't take advantage of my . . . unfortunate position."

"Hah!" He laughed heartily. "You, a damsel in distress!" The idea was so funny to him that he leaned against the wall and laughed, despite her icy stare.

"I hope you're enjoying yourself," she said coldly, trying to quell his mirth. "You're the one who locked us in here, you know. It certainly wasn't my idea. I didn't even invite you back!"

"Actually, you did," he retorted, taking the hammer out of her hand. He went to work with the wedge, talking over the pounding noises he was making. "You said I could measure the statue before you auctioned it off. And that's exactly what I intend to do before I leave—if I ever get out of here." He gave one more hard bang, sending the wedge right through the door, leaving a gaping hole. "Well, now we're getting somewhere," he added, obviously quite pleased with himself as he leaned down to examine his handiwork.

"My door!" she exclaimed. "Look what you've done to it!"

"Well, if you want to be out of here before the sun comes up," he said, reaching deftly through the hole with the hammer in his hand, "you'll just have to live with it." He pounded on the outside knob and then pulled at it with all of his strength. Sabrina watched as he exerted every ounce of effort, tugging until the lock suddenly broke off. The knob clattered to the floor as the door flew open, Colin falling back onto the bathroom floor.

He sat up slowly and looked at her. "At least your door will never get stuck again."

"Are you all right?" she asked.

He stood up to his full, lanky height. "I think so," he said ruefully. "No broken bones."

"I—I'll just go and put some clothes on." She stepped around him and walked out of the bathroom, acutely conscious that she was still only barely covered by the towel. Somehow, out of the close, steamy environment of the bathroom, she felt even more vulnerable. Fortunately her loft was L-shaped, and she disappeared around the corner with as much dignity as she could muster.

Colin watched her retreat, his eyes candidly assessing her graceful walk and the long, shapely legs that descended beneath the towel. She was uniquely beautiful. He couldn't deny it. He only wished she weren't so flighty.

Turning his attention to *Lady in Flight*, now striking and alone in the center of the room, he reached for the tools he had brought with him. In a moment he was completely engrossed as he measured the fossil from the statue's leg, up through its bottom, and around to the breast. A pocket calculator sat on the floor next to him, and he reached for it from time to time, quickly scribbling the results of his figuring on a pad.

Sabrina appeared a few minutes later, treading silently on bare feet and clothed in a blue and white caftan. She stood over him, watching curiously. His perfect concentration reminded her of her own when she was thoroughly involved in creating a work of art, and she couldn't help feeling a twinge of respect for his dedication. She crouched down next to him and offered a tentative smile. "Is it the missing link?"

His returning smile was appreciative. "As a matter of fact, it might be. Not between apes and man, but between amphibians and reptiles." Sabrina didn't quite know what he meant, but that breathless excitement of his had returned. Perhaps this really was some kind of scientific find.

She tried to look cogent about it, but he caught the flash of doubt in her eyes and explained, "Amphibians evolved into reptiles. This fellow falls right in the middle of that process."

"Oh," she frowned. "And when did all this happen?"

"About three hundred million years ago," he answered briefly.

"I see."

And she did see. As much as she hated to admit it, even to herself, she could see why he was so interested in this thing. The sheer age of it was awesome, and to think that it had survived all this time only to turn up in her sculpture!

"Is the whole skeleton there?" she asked.

He sat back on his heels and looked at her. "That's what I don't know. If it is . . ." He shook his head. "If it is, then this statue of yours will be worth its weight in gold. Intact fossils of this kind are extremely rare."

"Well," she said uneasily, "I suppose we'll never know, will we?"

His expression changed, and she knew that she was in for another confrontation.

All of his enthusiasm, the boyish wonder, and the precise calculations became directed into a single line of energy that had the force of a tidal wave. She could almost feel the determination that radiated from his clear blue eyes.

"We could know," Colin replied quietly, but his voice was somehow commanding, as if he knew he would get what he wanted.

"No, we can't," she snapped. "They're coming to pick up *Lady in Flight* tomorrow—"

"I know all about tomorrow," he cut in. "But meanwhile, it's still tonight. And tonight we can accomplish a great deal."

"Look, Mr. Forrester . . ." she began.

The steel never diminished, but he smiled and

said, "Please. Whenever I have the privilege of seeing a lady in her bathtub, I insist on being called Colin." His charm was devastating, and Sabrina wondered nervously why she hadn't noticed it before. Had it always been there, or did he only turn it on when he needed it? Or had she been too stubborn to see it?

"Well, Colin," she tried again. "I agreed to let you come up here and take your measurements. But anything else is out of the question. This is my property you're talking about, and I simply refuse to let anyone scrape at it, even in the name of science." She felt a little better after that speech, but he waved her objection aside.

"You're quite right, of course," he said soothingly. "I know you've worked very hard on this piece, and I know how much it means to you." He paused to gauge her reaction, and she looked at him suspiciously. "Fortunately, scraping won't be necessary."

Sabrina shifted uncomfortably. Despite his new cooperative attitude, she had the distinct feeling that his calculating mind was scheming rapidly. He had the predatory air of a lion about to go in for the kill, and the steel had only sharpened in his eyes, despite his casual attitude.

"There is another way," he continued. "X ray."

"What?" Now she was truly surprised. She had no idea what he was talking about, and this wasn't the first time he had baffled her by jumping to another subject without warning. Her attitude changed as she struggled to perceive his meaning.

"We can X-ray the statue without harming it," he explained in the same persuasive tone.

"How? By taking it to a hospital?"

"No," he smiled. "We have the facilities right in the museum."

"That's all very nice," she said faintly. "But the statue is being picked up tomorrow. It's here now and the museum is closed."

"None of which matters," he countered swiftly. "We can carry the statue downstairs and drive to the museum tonight. I have the keys."

"But that's—" She left the sentence deliberately unfinished, to show how outlandish she thought the whole idea was.

"That's what?" he pressed calmly. "Impossible? Hardly. It would only take a little while, and I'd have the answer to a question that could plague me and the rest of the scientific community for the rest of my life. You don't want that on your conscience, do you?"

She searched for a return to a reasonable, middle ground. "It's simply not my responsibility. I can't possibly take the risk," she protested.

"But what harm will it do?" he insisted. "None. There's no reason to be stubborn about it."

"Stubborn!" Her temper flared again, and she deliberately looked away from his riveting gaze. "Why on earth should I agree to this crazy scheme? It might make you and the rest of your crackpot friends happy, but it won't make me happy. There isn't one good reason why I should go along with you."

"Oh, yes there is," he said. "After all, I do have something you want. And this will cost you nothing."

"What could you possibly have that I want?" she asked scathingly.

"Have you forgotten already? The Lloyd's windows. I can't promise that we'll be able to transport every model you want, but we can try."

"Well . . ." The minute she hesitated, they both knew she had given in. "But—but how are we going to move my sculpture?" she asked plaintively. "It wouldn't exactly fit into the backseat of a cab."

"I have a truck downstairs," he beamed. "Do we have a deal?"

Her mouth fell open. "You have a truck? How convenient."

"Yes," he agreed, a triumphant grin spreading rapidly from ear to ear. "I never go anywhere without it.
Now what do you say? Do we have a deal?" He held
out his hand in a show of good faith. Once again she
noticed the scar, and he chuckled to himself. "Don't
worry," he said. "I won't let anything bite you."

Sabrina shook his hand warily. "It's not a dinosaur
I'm afraid of."

The ride uptown to the Museum of Natural History
was a memorable one for a number of reasons. First,
Sabrina insisted on riding in the back of the pickup
with *Lady in Flight*, and she bravely clutched the
statue as the truck bounced mercilessly over the potholes. Second, Colin insisted on maintaining a break-
neck speed, shouting through the open back
window, "Everyone in New York drives this way."
And third, Sabrina had to withstand the unusual cat-
calls of various late-night strollers and vagrants who
caught glimpses of her from the open end of the truck
as she held onto her statue for dear life.

To make matters worse, Colin kept up a continual
stream of chatter, almost as if he were baiting her.
"You're pretty quiet back there!" he shouted as they
bounced along.

"This is hardly a time for conversation!" she hollered back.

"Relax!" he said. "Everything will be just fine."

The truck careened around a corner and Sabrina
fought to keep her balance. "Scout's honor?" she
gasped.

He laughed. "Sure. Scout's honor."

The sidewalks were thronged with people, even at
this late hour, and a group of young men in leather
jackets stopped to watch the truck and its interesting
cargo.

"Hey, lady!" one of them called. "How come you're hugging that statue? You can hug me any time!"

Sabrina winced at the raucous laughter that followed, and Colin, sympathizing with her precarious position, said, "Hang on. We're almost there."

He cut around to the back of the huge, imposing museum, pulling into a small parking lot that was reserved for associates and employees. It was very dark, and Sabrina could see nothing except the ghostly branches of trees and the sliver of moon that glowed through the clouds. The truck jolted to a stop.

"Here we are!" Colin called. "Last stop!"

Sabrina sighed with resignation. It looked like the evening had only begun.

They walked up to a side door and Colin rang the night bell. A solitary watchman came to open it, and he greeted Colin by name before disappearing back into the gloomy depths of the empty museum.

"Are we going to have to lug my sculpture very far?" Sabrina asked worriedly.

"We're not going to lug it at all," he assured her. "We can use one of the forklifts. You go ahead inside and I'll meet you. It will take me awhile to get it ready."

Sabrina stepped inside. The first thing that hit her was the warm, musky smell of the museum. It was an old smell, but it was eminently comfortable, reminding her fleetingly of grade school trips and rainy Sunday outings.

"It's all right, George!" Colin called to the night watchman, his voice bouncing off the walls. "She's with me."

Colin disappeared into the darkness without another word, striding confidently through the endless galleries. Sabrina stepped forward into the Hall of Mammals and peered into the cavernous gloom. She could barely make out the large glass cases, each filled with stuffed mammals of every description and surrounded by lifelike reproductions of their natural environments. Long, smooth benches were spaced around the large room, and she sat down on one, too intimidated to go any further. Directly across from her, a gigantic black bear stood up on its hind legs in a woody setting, its mouth open and its eyes glittering, suspended forever in time. The bear looked at Sabrina and Sabrina looked at the bear, and suddenly she wondered what she was doing here at this crazy hour.

Her thoughts seemed enlarged in this weird setting, and she began to imagine all of the animals coming to life and dancing clumsily around the room. Her imagination would have run rampant, but she was interrupted by the sound of voices from the inner gallery.

"We'll just be a little while," Colin was saying to the watchman, and she caught the low hum of a hydraulic forklift buzzing through the hall. The sound grew louder, and she looked up, amazed, at the sight of Colin casually driving a contraption that held her statue on a platform. He drove right up to her bench and stopped.

"Hop aboard," he said cheerfully.

She clambered up next to him and he shifted into gear. Together they rode slowly through the museum, past displays of magnificent animals, Indian totem poles, and antique artifacts. It was like traveling on some sort of other-wordly journey, but Colin didn't seem to notice. They rode along, the statue leading the way, until they came to a huge elevator. He drove right inside it, pressed the button for the fourth floor, and sat back as they ascended.

Sabrina was practically speechless, but Colin was completely at home here. Before, they had been on her turf. Now they were on his.

"This isn't so bad, is it?" he asked mildly.

"That depends."

"On what?" He smiled. "Don't spoil things, Sabrina. We were getting along so well."

His use of her name seemed strangely intimate in this odd setting. She tried to brush it aside. "Were we? I suppose so."

"You know," he said thoughtfully, but with a glint in his eye, "you're not bad at all when you're not being so . . ." What was that word her friend Zeebo had used so candidly? "Affected," he finished.

"Affected? I thought you wanted to get along!" She tried to glare at him, but her expression was lost in the shadows.

"Oh, come off it, Sabrina. That pseudo-intellectual, pseudo-arty business."

"It's not fake," she retorted with justifiable anger. "That's exactly who I am."

The elevator arrived at the fourth floor with a little bump, and in a moment they were driving again, this time down a long hallway.

"All right," he continued affably. "You're just a nut, then. A bona fide, card-carrying nut."

"How flattering."

He shrugged. "I can't help it if I tell the truth. I'm a scientist, you know. I'm not interested in illusions."

"And what makes you think I'm an illusion?"

"Because," he answered simply, "you're too unreal to be true. People like you simply don't exist. Face it, Sabrina, SoHo is a gathering place, not a home. I bet you grew up in a hopelessly middle-class home, with mom and dad and apple pie. Am I right?" His smile was very self-assured.

Sabrina felt like hitting him on the head. "You couldn't be more wrong," she said crushingly, and she did nothing to hide the satisfaction in her voice. "For your information, Mr. Scientist, I was born in Greenwich Village. I grew up there. People do live there, you know, and they even have children. My mother is a jazz singer and my father writes boys' adventure stories." She stopped, cataloguing her resentment of his smug remark. "So the next time you go in search of great truths, I'd suggest you do your research first."

She fully expected him to be angry, or sorry, or even embarrassed, but all he did was to throw back his head and laugh delightedly. "Well said, Ms. Melendey. I must say, I am surprised. The genuine article, eh?"

They came to a halt, and Colin switched on a light. Sabrina squinted against the instant glare, too taken aback by the odd sight in front of her to say anything at first. They were in the Hall of the Dinosaurs. Huge skeletons stood throughout the room, some of them over a hundred feet long. Their jaws were set into eerie grins, almost as if they were smiling an outlandish welcome.

Sabrina's eyes grew wide as she stared. She had been here many years ago, but she had forgotten just how large these skeletons were, and how complex. Each one was composed of a myriad of bones, and the display was obviously a masterpiece, one of the showcases of the museum. Colin snuck a glance at her and saw that she was properly impressed. He drove past the exhibit, naming each dinosaur as they went along. When they got to the tyrannosaurus, he laughed, looking first at his hand and then at Sabrina.

She gazed in awe at the imposing skeleton, her eyes lingering on the jaw. "You got your hand caught in one of these?" she asked, her voice barely more than a whisper. He nodded. "You're lucky you still have your hand."

They reached the workroom and drove inside, Colin slowly lowering the statue to the floor. Sabrina's eyes were everywhere. It looked like the shop on the set of a monster movie, and she smiled absently as she thought of Mishi. Half-formed skeletons were everywhere, and a few skulls lolled casually on a wooden table. Tools of all kinds were hung on the wall. Colin wheeled *Lady in Flight* over to a large machine in the corner, positioning her carefully. He pressed a few buttons, a few lights flashed, and it was all over.

"That's it?" Sabrina asked.

"Disappointed? I'm sorry I couldn't give you more of a show."

"Oh, it's pretty entertaining here," she said dryly. "I just can't believe that's all there was to it."

He sat on the edge of the work table and smiled at her. He seemed relaxed now, and his eyes were candid and direct. "We still have to develop the X rays."

She was startled. "Now?"

"Why not?"

"Because it's almost two in the morning, that's why! And I've got a big day tomorrow."

"Take it easy," he said lazily. "We had a deal, remember?"

Sabrina was disconcerted. Colin's drive to find out what was in the limestone seemed to have vanished. Perhaps it was because he had the statue in his territory now, and he was in control. But whatever the reason, he folded his arms and looked at her with frank appreciation, and she found his boldness unsettling. Before, it had been convenient to peg him as the insensitive mad scientist. But suddenly he didn't seem that way, and she had trouble remembering exactly why she had found him so distasteful.

Or had she? As she looked at him now, she saw the tiny lines at the corners of his mouth, and the crinkles around his eyes that always made him seem to be laughing at some private joke. His hair was disheveled, but attractively so, as if he had just spent the night— She caught herself in her own thoughts and almost blushed. All at once, completely unbidden, came a new question. What would it be like to kiss this man? She stared at him, her eyes roaming over the asymmetrical but very strong features of his provocatively intelligent face. When she realized that he knew she was staring fixedly at his mouth, she dropped her glance immediately.

"Are you going to develop those X rays now?" she asked, to change the subject.

He smiled a baffling little smile, scooped up the X rays, and disappeared into an adjoining darkroom. Sabrina looked around her uneasily. She was alone in a very odd room full of skeletons in the middle of the night. But then she noticed a desk in the corner. She hadn't seen it before, probably because the rest of the room was so startling. It looked like a perfectly ordinary desk—neat, well-organized, and furnished with a typewriter and a phone. Walking over to it, she realized that it was Colin's desk. In fact, this crazy room appeared to be his office! What a place to work, she thought, glancing down at some of the memos that had been left on the desk. *Call Dr. Chin in Shanghai. Lecture at Princeton—3:30. Lloyd's exhibit. Call artist again. Review list of items. Order more glue.*

The list was long and Sabrina felt a twinge of guilt that she had inadvertantly, through her irresponsibility, increased the sum of his many responsibilities.

Lost in thought, she wandered out of the room and into the great hall filled with motionless, timeless dinosaurs. The tyrannosaurus stood alone and magnificent in the center, and she went over to look at it.

She then wandered over to the stegosaurus, and reached out to touch one of the spikes that protruded from the tail. It was as smoothly worn as a priceless antique—which was exactly what it was. Walking down the length of the skeleton, she stopped again to examine the head. The mouth was open, as if the animal were about to lean down and take a bite out of her.

"Careful, big fellow," she warned jovially. "I just might bite back."

Moving on, she paused to examine some drawings in a glass case. One of them was labeled "Seymouria."

"Seymour's relatives," she murmured to herself. That's what Colin had been talking about in her loft. The fossil in her sculpture was some kind of relative to this seymouria creature.

"Hello there, Seymour," she offered. "Did you know that your cousin Roger is in the next room, trapped inside a statue?"

"Not cousin," Colin's voice said from the doorway. "Try grandson. Or better yet, great-grandson. We'll know as soon as the negatives are dry."

He walked toward her, a smile on his face. "And good news—we should be able to provide you with just about everything you requested."

"There, you see?" she asked smugly. "It wasn't so outlandish after all, was it?"

He shrugged. "We'll see. But your attitude *was* pretty outrageous. You never answered my calls. You didn't even open my letter until tonight. If you had been willing to discuss it sensibly, I wouldn't have written that letter. Besides, I wasn't even sure what you wanted. Your list was so long that I was afraid you wanted the dinosaur skeletons."

"How could you think I would want those huge things?" Sabrina asked. "Do you think the shoppers at Lloyd's would be interested in the authenticity of a bunch of old bones? Besides, they wouldn't fit in the store, let alone the windows."

He looked at her shrewdly and saw that she was sincere. The realization hurt him a little. Old bones were the mainstay of his career. They spoke of eras and scenarios that had disappeared millions of years ago—mute but vibrant testimony to the turbulent adolescence of the earth. Sabrina had called him insensitive, but she was oblivious to her own insensitivity, and to the triumph of exploration that this room represented. Her eyes clouded as she caught his stare, as if she knew that something was wrong. But all she said was, "I'm glad we've cleared this up."

"Good," he said briefly, still studying her face. It was difficult to look too long at that face, because its ethereal beauty enchanted him. He realized that he was ogling her like a schoolboy, and Colin reminded himself once again that her outward beauty did not seem to match her cold thoughts. "Come on," he said. "Those X rays should be dry enough to examine."

She followed him back to his office, and he went into the darkroom, emerging with three large negatives. He placed them on a screen that lined one wall and then flicked on the light. The negatives revealed the stark silhouette of her statue, but it was what was inside the statue that made both of them catch their breath.

A complete skeleton was lodged neatly and precisely inside the sleek contours of *Lady in Flight*. Not only was it an eerily outlandish sight, but there was something vaguely familiar about it. Sabrina stared in awe at the outline, her mind darting back to the glass cases in the room outside.

"Seymouria!" she exclaimed.

He lifted an eyebrow, impressed by her powers of observation. "Not a bad try," he commented. "I'm surprised you noticed it. Actually, it's a close relative—"

"Well, I am an artist, you know," she answered, trying to sound modest, and failing. "I . . . look at things a lot."

But Colin wasn't listening. He was staring raptly at the X rays, doing some kind of complex figuring in his head and mumbling the results out loud. "Incredible," he finished in a voice filled with wonder. He ran over to the screen and examined the pictures once more, this time with minute scrutiny. "Incredible!" Suddenly he dashed over to his desk and began rummaging in a drawer.

"What are you looking for?" Sabrina asked.

Papers spilled onto the desk, and he shoved them aside. "I'm looking for an old sketch I made when I was at a museum in Ontario. It's a drawing of—" He found it suddenly, crying "Aha!" and holding it triumphantly up to the light.

Sabrina leaned over and peered at it, her expression an interesting mixture of curiosity and trepidation. "A foot!" she pronounced, staring at it. "I'm looking at a foot."

Colin nodded enthusiastically, still poring through his desk and tossing items impatiently aside. "But not just any foot," he added judiciously. "This foot is the only one if its kind!" With that, he ran back to the X rays, still illuminated on the far wall.

Sabrina followed him, not sure if she really wanted to know what was going on, but knowing that his enthusiasm was going to stimulate her curiosity until she would *have* to know.

Picking up a magnifying glass, he examined the X rays once more, comparing them to the sketch in his hand. "Incredible," he repeated. "Absolutely incredible."

She was beginning to feel left out. "All this excitement over a stupid foot?" she asked, trying to bring him back to earth.

Colin's eyes snapped as he looked at her. "Do you realize what we've got here?" he asked breathlessly.

"No. I don't," she replied. "I certainly wish you'd enlighten me."

"It's all there!" he explained simply.

"*What's* all there?" Getting solid information out of him was like pulling teeth.

"An entire fossil, completely intact, right here in this statue! And not just any fossil! Its foot matches my drawing . . . it has to be! Oh, what a find!"

"You're saying this thing is, uh, rare?" she asked carefully.

"Rare? *Rare?*" Colin was so excited that he was hopping up and down, unable to contain his joy. "It's a rogericus! It's the only one of its kind! Nothing else like it exists!" He threw his arms up into the air and began an impromptu waltz around the cluttered room, his long legs carrying him gracefully as he spun around.

"But—but what about that foot?" she asked helplessly.

"That's the whole point!" he said, sliding to a stop in front of her. "Before, all we had was that one foot. But now—now we have the whole thing!" He was about to take off again, but her look stopped him.

"Do you mean to tell me that a priceless scientific find is parked inside my sculpture?" Her voice was incredulous.

He nodded vigorously, his clear blue eyes shining.

"And it's related to that . . . Seymour thing outside?" she continued.

He spun around in a carefree circle, his arms forming a joyous arc. "Related? I'll say they're related! Just look at them! It's a missing link! The proverbial missing link! What we have here, my dear Sabrina, is a virtual family reunion!" When she still looked puzzled, Colin calmed down enough to explain further. "Don't you get it? That's why I thought the limestone came from Ontario. That's where that foot was found. I don't know how this creature got himself stuck in the Adirondacks, but I guess it doesn't matter. After all, he's the first of his kind ever to be found intact." That one word brought his joyous enthusiasm back with a renewed surge of energy. "Intact!"

Once more he was leaping and prancing around the room, Sabrina smiling politely as she watched him. She was glad about his discovery . . . but she worried about *Lady in Flight*.

Colin was oblivious to any sense of reason. He was now dancing a sort of Irish jig, his feet springing nimbly as he sang an impromptu tune. "Oh, the foot bone's connected to the leg bone . . . and the leg bone's connected to the thigh bone . . ." He danced over to the work table and threw the piece of paper with the sketch up into the air. It floated down rhythmically, landing squarely atop a lone skull. Sabrina laughed, amusement overtaking her fears for a moment as she surveyed the outlandish scene.

Colin stopped suddenly and looked at her appreciatively. Her eyes lit up when she laughed, and the sound was gracefully fluent, like clear water cascading down a green hill. Her teeth were small and very white, and the delicately etched lines of her face seemed to dance for an instant as he stared at her. The blue and white caftan rested easily on her small frame, and all at once he noticed the elusive curves underneath that had been so artfully camouflaged before. She seemed utterly mercurial, a free spirit always in motion who had paused only long enough to shower him with the intoxicating lilt of her laughter.

"God, you're beautiful," he said suddenly, surprising both of them.

Sabrina looked down at the floor, and when nothing happened, she slowly looked up again. Although embarrassed, Colin was still staring at her with that intent, provocative look, and the silence between them seemed ready to overflow with anticipation. The sheer joy of discovery in Colin's eyes had not faded, but it was no longer clear what had caused it. Sabrina stood mesmerized as the space between them narrowed and then closed. His hands moved quickly to her shoulders, holding her gently, and his mouth met hers in a kiss that seemed filled with tender decision. I've decided to kiss you, it said, and now that I am, there's no turning back.

But it ended before she had time to savor it. Her eyes, which had fluttered to a close, flew open as she searched his face for a clue. Was he toying with her? Why hadn't he continued?

"What was that for?" she whispered, a shadow of doubt crossing her face.

He reacted instantly, letting his hands drop from her shoulders. "Scientific inquiry," he answered too quickly.

Sabrina did not know why he had stopped. She knew only that the fleeting kiss was the sweetest, most tantalizing one she had ever tasted. Her own resolve strengthened as she decided in one determined instant that she could not rest until she had tasted more. Standing up on her toes to reach him, she gently cupped his face in her slender hands and kissed him carefully and tenderly on the mouth, taking all the time in the world. Sure enough, that same piercing sweetness enveloped her, and this time she let it weave its magic before she lowered herself back to the floor.

Colin looked down at her. His heart was fluttering and he was deliciously confused. "And what was that for?" he murmured.

A tiny smile curved across her face. "Artistic temperament," she answered.

He said nothing more, but he wrapped his arms around her and drew her close. They stared at each other for one breathless moment, and then their mouths met again in a kiss that trembled with a nameless yearning. Sabrina, who usually hid any insecurity beneath her zany exterior, was suddenly stripped of all defenses as she sank under his spell. Had it been only a short while ago that she had wondered what it would be like to kiss this man? Now she was actually kissing him, and she reflected distractedly that the reality far exceeded her own curious fantasy.

Sabrina was able to charm people and was used to getting her way. She knew how to wind her distinct femininity around her buoyant spirit and disarm most people. She had flattered herself that she had managed to do this with Colin, but as he gently and firmly parted her lips with his tongue to explore the warm interior of her mouth with sensual deliberation, she felt for the first time that this strategy had accomplished far more than she had intended. The warm sweetness was almost unbearable, and the only way to make it bearable was to taste more. Her arms unconsciously went around his neck, her hands lacing together and then restlessly unfolding as her fingers stroked the sensitive skin at the back of his neck.

She was swept along on a current that was much too strong for her, but she didn't care. Nothing mattered except his electric hold on her, and she wanted it to go on forever. His hands moved sensuously to the small of her back and relished the mold of her hips, his fingers spreading apart to hold them. Sabrina swayed slightly, igniting him even further as the curves of her body moved under his hands, and he gripped her tightly in response, crushing her delicate breasts against his chest.

Her eyes never opened, even when the first few kisses ended. His mouth explored the soft line of her cheek, descending to her pert chin and then to her narrow throat. She knew that any moment she was going to let out a helpless moan, and when it came, he gently parted the deep opening at the neck of the caftan and stroked the smooth, pale skin above her breasts.

"You are an elf," he whispered savagely. "A beguiling little elf."

Sabrina could barely speak, but she managed to whisper, "Hold me again."

He obliged her by drawing her near again, but he did not enfold her in his arms. He kept her only a fraction of an inch from his body while his hands played along the opening of the caftan, finally reaching down to hold her breasts. A small, masculine sound of satisfaction escaped him as he found what he sought. They were small but very firm, standing up of their own accord to meet him with a slight quiver. He closed his eyes and savored the soft, intimate sensation, before drawing his hands back to gently stroke the pale pink nipples.

The white heat of desire shot through Sabrina's body so that she was no longer sure she could stand on her feet. Her knees had weakened dangerously, and her eyes opened reluctantly.

His eyes were blazing blue fire. As he continued to tease her breasts, Colin murmured, "I can't believe I met you. This is the greatest day of my life."

Even through the blinding passion flooding her, she was surprised. "Really?" she asked, unable to say any more.

"Really." He was serious. "Not only do I get to make love to an enchanting woman, but I discover something that will be the find of the decade."

She wasn't prepared for that. It was hardly the sort of thing she fancied a man should say while he was making love to her. "Never mind that now . . ." she whispered, closing her eyes and pressing against him. "Tomorrow is the auction . . ."

He started at her words, and Sabrina could have bitten her tongue off. She had been trying to move his focus on the statue from science to art, but all she succeeded in doing was to spark his interest once again.

"Yes," he murmured, his voice growing stronger. "After the auction the rogericus will definitely have a home. Here."

This time her eyes opened wide and a flash of suspicion shot across her face. "What do you mean?" she asked, more sharply than she had intended.

He looked surprised, and his hands finally halted their tantalizing movements. "Well, you don't think I'm going to let a find like that go."

"I thought you were finished with it! You found what you were looking for, didn't you?"

"Well, yes, but now that I've found it, I have to study it. I'll have to submit a complete report—"

"What!" she stepped back, her whole body trembling.

Colin was trembling too, but was not about to lose his ground. "That fossil has to be studied carefully, inch by inch. The only way to do that is to scrape painstakingly—"

"Scrape! Are you serious?" she shouted.

"Look, Sabrina," he said hastily. "I'll buy the statue if that's what you want. But I've got to have it at any cost. We may have to remove the fossil altogether."

Her eyes flashed defiantly. "Over my dead body," she retorted, meaning it. They stared at each other, their hunger slowly ebbing, replaced by anger. "I spent months on that piece of sculpture. It's the turning point of my career."

"I know that," he stated calmly. "But what you don't understand is that I can easily make you a copy of it, right here. Free of charge, of course. You can have it in any medium you want. Bronze, clay . . . even gold," he added, half-jokingly.

Sabrina was not amused. "You are the most infuriating man I have ever met. I don't want a copy of my work. The original is worth ten copies." She held up her hand, anticipating his reaction. "Which doesn't mean you're invited to make ten copies. The whole point is that the work is unique. I can't sell a copy. Whoever buys it will own something that is one of a kind.

"Enough," she proclaimed backing away. "I'm leaving." Before he had time to stop her, she ran over to the forklift and jumped into the driver's seat. She got it started by sheer instinct, letting it roll forward menacingly as he leaped out of the way. She ran over a few books and papers that were scattered on the floor, heading with determination toward *Lady in Flight*.

"Be careful!" he shouted, chasing after her. "What the hell do you think you're doing?"

"I'm taking my sculpture home!" she shouted back. "I've wasted enough time here." She came to an abrupt halt in front of the statue. "I'm sorry to take your new toy away from you, but it is mine, after all."

"Let me do that, for heaven's sake," he insisted, grabbing her arm and staring her in the face. "Just let me position it properly," he said, moving toward the statue. He tripped over the forklift and fell against the statue, causing it to veer dangerously to one side.

"Now you've done it!" she cried, jumping down and rushing to balance the heavy sculpture which teetered precariously in the other direction.

"Oh, my God!" she exclaimed. "Quick! Do something!"

Colin wrapped his muscular arms around the statue and held it fast, easing it slowly but firmly back to its original position. Small beads of sweat stood out on his forehead, and for a long moment neither of them said a word. He avoided looking at her, missing her utterly crestfallen expression. The crisis averted, he finally straightened up, but his hand flew to the small of his back.

"My back!" he hollered. He bent over again, obviously fighting the pain.

"Oh, no!" Sabrina ran over and tried to help him stand up, but he waved her away as if she were a fly.

"Don't you touch me!" he growled. "You've done enough!"

"But I can help," she insisted. "I have this friend who does Japanese massage, and—"

"I don't want to hear about it. Just leave me alone," he said between clenched teeth. "Everything you touch turns into a disaster area. Your bathroom door, your oven—how you get through life without falling through trapdoors is a mystery to me."

She backed away, intimidated. "I'm sorry about your back," she offered quietly. "And thank you for saving my sculpture."

He grimaced, and she stepped forward quickly, placing her hands firmly on his hips. "Breathe deeply," she commanded.

"I'm not—"

"Just do it," she insisted. beginning a slow, careful massage of the injured area. He stopped resisting and relaxed, letting her gentle, pliant fingers work their magic. Eventually, he was able to stand straight again, inching upwards by degrees as a slow smile of relief spread across his face.

"That's better," he breathed. "Definitely better."

Sabrina's hands continued to massage his lean, hard muscles. "You should be more careful," she admonished, but her tone was sympathetic.

"I know," he agreed. "It always does this. That statue of yours must really have been out for revenge."

She let her hands drop, and there was a pause, during which Colin secretly wished she would continue and Sabrina felt a sudden tug of longing that she couldn't suppress.

"Well . . ." she said at last. "I guess we'd better get going. This doesn't look like a very nice place to spend the night. I wouldn't want to wake up and see a skull staring at me."

He laughed a little. "Couldn't you just leave the statue here overnight and have it picked up in the morning? It really is a back-breaker, you know."

Sabrina hesitated. "Sorry," she said. "But the auction house is scheduled to pick it up at my place, and it's too late to change the plans. Besides, I'm not leaving it here by itself, and that's that."

"Oh, all right," he sighed. "Come on, I'll take you home."

Getting the statue back onto the forklift and out of the museum was no problem, but getting it up the stairs to Sabrina's loft was a slow and painstaking procedure. When at last the heavy piece of sculpture was resting once again in its original spot, Colin heaved a loud sign of relief.

"Whew!" he exclaimed, wiping his forehead with one arm. "Next time, try sculpting a midget."

Sabrina yawned. "Do you know what time it is?"

"Three-thirty," he replied, glancing at his watch.

"Well," she said, "I think I'll go right to bed." Her choice of words made him glance at her with quizzical interest, and she hastily added, "I'm bushed, and I have a lot to do tomorrow. Thanks again for bringing me home."

The silence that followed was almost tangible as they stood and looked at each other, suddenly very shy. They were both too tired to engage in any more heated discussions about the fate of the statue, and neither one of them had forgotten the passion that had erupted so unexpectedly, only to be so sharply interrupted.

"Thank you," Colin answered at last. "I must say, it's been an experience." He walked around the statue once, stopping to pat its bottom fondly. "Good-bye, old friend," he said. "And I mean very, very old friend."

Sabrina shifted from one foot to the other. "Uh—I'll see you out," she offered, but suddenly he was standing directly in front of her, his lean, tall body towering over her petite form.

"Sabrina," he whispered. His soft utterance of her name sent a little shiver through her blood. She looked up very slowly, because she knew what would happen when she did. His face was hard and yet open, and the glint in his blue eyes told her that he wanted her in a way that thrilled and frightened her all at once. When he took her in his arms, she wasn't sure what she wanted, but there was no time to think about it. Colin's mouth sought hers demandingly, and the charge of sweet electricity that went through her obliterated all thoughts of protest. It made no sense, she thought brokenly, as the kiss deepened and consumed her. He wasn't at all the type of man she usually fell for. She had no business getting involved this way.

But his hands, the hands that had so meticulously and skillfully measured the contours of her statue, were now exploring the warm, yielding contours of her body, and they evoked such a deep, burning response that she was shocked by her own abandon. Never had anyone elicited such driving passion from her so easily. He kissed her smooth cheek, her ear, and the side of her neck, leaving a trail of glowing honey that lingered and blended with each new touch. Sabrina moaned helplessly, scarcely aware that he was just as awash with desire as she was.

"Touch me," he commanded, holding her firmly by the hips and gazing down into her eyes.

She struggled to come down to earth. "Colin, I don't think—"

"That's right. Don't think about anything. Don't you see what's been happening all evening? God, Sabrina, you torment me! You're like a butterfly that I can't catch." He kissed her again with impetuous

need, and this time her hands gladly found their way
to the tight, hard lines of his chest, which she stroked
with her fingertips. He responded instantly, and she
was surprised to see the power she had over him.

His mouth found hers, gently at first with tiny nib-
bles that teased her into aggression. She moved her
head back to receive him completely, and he
explored the interior of her mouth as he reached for
the lush, satiny peaks that fit so easily into his hands.
Her soft, pale nipples started at his touch, and once
again she was amazed at how quickly he could fire
her with passion. It was so easy with him, so very
easy to lose herself in a whirlpool of sensation that
had no beginning and no end.

Sabrina trembled visibly as Colin pressed her
against him hungrily. "You are a very beautiful
women," he whispered huskily, "but you'll be even
more beautiful when I can see all of you, have all of
you. I want to make you flame for me, Sabrina. Trust
me. . . ."

She did trust him, but she didn't know why. All
she knew was that her body was tingling with
breathless anticipation exceeded only by the certainty that his lovemaking would be like nothing she
had ever experienced before.

He kissed her once more, teasing her and igniting
her until his own desire was almost unbearable, and
then, without lifting his mouth from hers, he bent
and swooped her up in his arms. Excruciating pain
registered immediately in his face as he grabbed the
small of his back.

"Oh, no, not again!" he cried as Sabrina slid to the
floor, leaning against him.

She looked up at him in alarm and said, "Something tells me this was not meant to be." Within seconds she was massaging the injured area, but this
time it did no good. She gave up, hit with a sudden
inspiration.

"All right," she announced, as she headed over to the closet and pulled out what appeared to be a rolled-up canvas. "Tonight you'll sleep samurai-style." She unrolled it onto the floor and gestured hospitably. "By yourself," she added.

He looked from her to the floor mat and back again.

"That's all I need," he muttered, still clutching his back. "I think I'll stick to a real bed, if you don't mind." He looked around expectantly, his expression becoming slowly mystified. His puzzled gaze took in the desk, a table, and a few chairs, but one necessary item was glaringly absent. "Uh, Sabrina . . . where is your bed, anyway?" She pointed to the unrolled mat on the floor. "You're looking at it."

As if he couldn't quite believe it, Colin's eyes traversed the room once more, as if looking for the bed that must be there.

"It's called a futon," she explained helpfully. "The Japanese have been using them for centuries. Try it," she urged, noting his sour expression.

"I'm in no mood for experiments," he pronounced grimly. "I need a firm, ordinary mattress."

"A futon *is* a firm mattress," she pointed out. "I promise you'll like it."

"I can't," he said stubbornly.

She sighed. "Well, I'm going into the kitchen to fix us both a nightcap. I think we need it. You can decide what to do."

Sabrina disappeared into the kitchen without another word, leaving Colin to contemplate the futon. It lay there placidly, a thick, plain rectangle, and he kicked it a few times to make sure it was solid. Frowning suspiciously, he eased himself onto it very gingerly. Then he turned and slowly lay down, stretching his long, lean body onto the supportive mat.

"Hmmm," he said judiciously, moving around cautiously. "Not bad. Not bad at all."

In the kitchen, Sabrina poured liqueur into two cordial glasses and placed them on a wicker tray. It was hard to believe that she was getting involved with a man who was probably, at this very moment, hobbling around her living room refusing to try something new. He was certainly a very strange man—brilliant and yet narrow-minded, unconventional, but unartistic, and undeniably attractive despite his infuriating views. All in all, he was a bundle of paradoxes that inexplicably combined to make him the most magnetic man she had ever met.

Sabrina picked up the tray, pushed through the swinging door, and marched back into the living room, but she was totally unprepared for the sight that met her eyes.

There, stretched out on the futon like a well-fed baby without a care in the world, was Mr. Magnetism, sound asleep.

Chapter Four

❧

Colin opened his eyes and focused on one of the paintings hanging on the wall. It depicted an unfamiliar bunch of flowers, and for a moment he did not know where he was. Then he turned and saw Sabrina's face, soft and vulnerable in repose. She was sleeping on another futon stretched out next to his, and she still wore the blue and white caftan. He looked down and saw that she had thrown an afghan over him.

Sitting up slowly, he was vaguely aware of a new sensation. He couldn't quite place it, and he got to his feet, drawing himself to his full height. What was it? He walked around the room very quietly, careful not to wake Sabrina, and suddenly he knew what it was.

His back didn't hurt. In fact, it felt better than it had in years. He lifted his arms over his head and stretched to the ceiling, reveling in a delicious feeling of well-being. Looking down at the futon with a new appreciation, he suppressed a laugh. Sabrina was different, all right, but he had to admit that she had a strange hold over him. It wasn't just her beauty, and it wasn't just the heady rush of passion that she had awakened in him—although the very memory of that made him flutter a little inside. She seemed so mercurial, and yet somehow she was as solid and stubborn as a rock. He could see the innate intelligence in her, yet she persisted in being narrow-minded to an irritating degree. She was wildly offbeat, but she had resolutely refused to sell her work at a low price, and her tenaciousness was going to pay off—today. All in all, she was a bundle of contradictions, and all he knew was that he wanted to penetrate her willowy shell and find the warm, willful woman inside.

Sabrina did not stir, and he hesitated to waken her. She still looked worn out. Casting one more long, lingering look at her extraordinary face, he tiptoed over to her desk, found a pencil and a piece of paper, and scribbled a hasty note: *"I'll call you. C."*

"I don't understand him at all," Sabrina said to Zeebo as they stood in one corner of the auction room later that day, watching as the bidders strolled in. "How can he be so madly in love with a stupid fossil?"

Zeebo smirked. "You can't fool me, Sabrina," he drawled. "I can tell you like him."

"Don't tell me you're on his side!" she admonished.

He shrugged. "Don't worry, love. In a few hours your sculpture will be in a new home, and your worries will be over."

Sabrina said nothing. She was too nervous to think about Colin. She was too nervous to think about anything at all, so she simply hung on to Zeebo and let him chatter away.

"Relax, will you?" he said, squeezing her arm and leading her over to some empty chairs at the side. "When this is over, I'm going to buy those paintings you did at my villa in the south of France last summer, and this time you're not going to stop me. I'll pay the going rate, and you can't possibly object to that."

Sabrina's eyes lit up with excitement. "Oh, Zeebo!" But then she faltered. "No. No, please, I want you to have them as a gift."

"Nonsense," he said briskly, straightening his bow

tie. "You're going to be famous now. Why should you give anything away? Whatever *Lady in Flight* gets today is what I'll pay for those paintings." He smiled ironically. "Your starving artist routine is about to end."

The room continued to fill and programs were distributed as the works of art were brought onto the small platform. Sabrina took a program and perused it anxiously. Much to her dismay, there were thirteen items up for auction, and hers was at the very end.

"Oh, no!" she groaned. "I'm last! By the time they get to me, everyone will have run out of money."

"No chance," Zeebo said. "Not this crowd. I'm probably the poorest person here, and I don't have a ceiling. You forget, this auction is by invitation only. Some of the most savvy art collectors in the world will be here. Exclusivity, Sabrina. It's the key to great wealth."

"Speaking of wealth," she said dryly, "look who's coming."

Zeebo turned and they both watched as Arthur Wellington entered the room, shook hands with various acquaintances and then headed in their direction.

"Good morning, Sabrina," he said warmly. "Congratulations."

"A bit premature, but thank you," she smiled. "I still have this terrible fear that when *Lady in Flight* goes on the block, there won't be a single bidder."

"Don't be silly," Wellington said heartily. "I intend to open the bidding myself." He paused. "There is one other thing that I hate to bring up at a time like this, but I'm afraid it can't wait. The Museum of Natural History called this morning." Sabrina's heart plunged, but she listened politely. "They have a warehouse full of items all ready to be sent over to the store. But they need your signature first, and your final approval. Do you think you can get to it today?"

"Oh, Arthur," Sabrina assured him sincerely, "It's perfectly all right. I've already spoken with Colin—I mean Mr. Forrester. I'll take care of it first thing tomorrow morning."

"But they said the items have to be shipped out by five o'clock this afternoon," he said worriedly. "I believe the humidity is bad for the models and they have to be inside the store by the end of the day. And it's supposed to rain tomorrow. But I'll leave it in your hands," he finished with a polite smile. Sabrina nodded, trying to look confident, and he sauntered off.

She watched him curiously, wondering what the reason was for the sudden rush. Just then, her eyes caught sight of Colin walking into the now-crowded room. He was dressed impeccably in a charcoal gray suit with a white shirt and burgundy tie. But instead of looking ultraconservative, he managed to look rakishly masculine, as if he were wearing those well-tailored clothes only for his own amusement.

"What's he doing here?" she wondered aloud. Colin saw her at once and made his way through the crowd, claiming the seat next to her. He nodded to Zeebo and then turned immediately to her.

"I came as soon as I could," he said in a conspiratorial whisper. Sabrina blinked. What was he talking about? She hadn't expected him to come. "I just finished studying those X rays I took last night, and—"

"How did you get in here?" she interrupted suspiciously. "This is a private auction."

Colin flipped open his wallet and flashed a New York City museum pass. "No one asked which museum I was with," he shrugged.

Her mouth dropped open. "But—but why are you here?"

"It's about your statue. The X rays. They—"

She held up her hand, ornamented by the snake bracelet on her wrist. "I don't want to hear any more about it. After today you can speak to the new owner."

"Well, he's going to be a very unhappy new owner when he discovers that his priceless statue might crack."

Sabrina was in no mood for this topic. Already the room was filled to capacity and newcomers had to stand on the side of the room. Photographers were taking pictures of the works of art and of the artists who waited nervously. A bulb flashed in Sabrina's face, and Colin continued.

"You don't understand," he insisted. "It has to do with weathering."

Sabrina was completely exasperated. "Well, the statue looks fine, and no one but you would ever notice such a stupid thing. Can't you ever think about anything else?" She turned away, refusing to discuss it further.

Colin was not about to back off, but the auctioneer came in from one side and everyone in the room hushed expectantly. The man approached the podium and checked the microphone as the last few people hurried inside. Sabrina's heart began to beat wildly in anticipation. This was it. For years, her life had been building up to this moment. Her palms pressed together, and she realized that they were as cold as ice.

Zeebo patted her arm reassuringly and she gave him a nervous smile. She caught Colin's dissatisfied, jumpy expression out of the corner of her eye, but ignored it, facing front with all the bravery she could muster.

The auction began with a painting of a can of Spam meat. The auctioneer gave a brief, persuasive speech, describing the artist's background and previous works. Then the bidding began.

"We'll start the bidding at two thousand dollars," he announced. "Do I hear two?" Someone in the audience gestured immediately, and the auctioneer continued with a slight nod. "Two, do I hear three thousand? Three . . . three . . . three! Do I hear four?" Again someone gestured, almost imperceptibly, and the man proceeded without missing a beat. "Four . . . four . . . do I hear five?" He looked around the room, pausing for only a split second—although Sabrina knew it must seem like eternity to the artist—and then said, "Four thousand. Going once, going twice . . ." One last pause, and then a bang of the gavel. "Sold! For four thousand dollars."

Scattered applause followed and Sabrina looked curiously around the room to locate the buyer, but no one stepped forward.

"Who bought it?" she asked impatiently, pinching Zeebo's arm. "I can't see anyone claiming it."

"Of course not," he answered loftily. "Most bidders in this group want to remain anonymous. They have special signals known only to the auctioneer."

"I know that," she said. "But why keep it a secret afterwards? I should think the new owner would want to gloat a little."

Zeebo smiled. "People don't necessarily want to acknowledge that they bought a new young talent until the artist becomes very famous. They don't want to be made to look foolish if the investment doesn't pan out. Besides, anonymity helps keep the prices down. When you can't see your competitor, you don't have any clues as to what he's thinking."

"But, Zeebo," Sabrina frowned, "all of the artists here are good. You know that. They wouldn't be here if they weren't."

"To a degree," Zeebo agreed. "But it takes a few years to weed out the A's and separate them from the A+'s. I firmly believe that last painting was an A+."

"You do? Then why didn't you bid for it?" Sabrina asked.

He smiled triumphantly. "I did, I did. In fact, I just bought it."

Sabrina gazed at him in astonishment, and Colin, who had listened to the whole exchange, laughed appreciatively.

The bidding continued as each object was brought onto the platform, its qualities and potential described. Sabrina watched the whole procedure in awe. She understood more than ever exactly how good she was, and this knowledge frightened her as much as it thrilled her. She was about to enter a whole new phase of her life, and there was no turning back. From now on, she would be a contender, someone to be reckoned with in the highly competitive art world.

All of the artists being auctioned today were young, but she was the youngest. All of them had struggled for years, and they had been picked from dozens of other worthy candidates. Sabrina said a silent prayer for *Lady in Flight* because she knew that the lady in flight was herself.

As the twelfth item was auctioned, she felt a new, last-minute sense of calm. It was too late to make any changes; there was no reason to be nervous. Whatever could have been done was done already. Accepting whatever would befall her with philosophical equilibrium, she sat back and listened to the now-familiar voice of the auctioneer as he coaxed the last few bids for the item before hers.

"Sixteen thousand . . . going once . . . going twice . . . seventeen? Thank you, I have seventeen thousand. Do I hear eighteen? Eighteen thousand? Seventeen, going once . . . going twice . . ." The gavel pounded. "Sold! For seventeen thousand dollars."

The applause accompanied the flash of cameras as the artist's picture was taken, and the last item was carted onto the platform. Sabrina felt a stab of poignancy as she looked at her work. After today, she might never see it again. Her eyes caressed it as no one else's could; she knew every line, every plane as intimately as she knew her own body. A rush of pride mingled with a ripple of pain. That was her baby up there. She fervently hoped that all would go well with it.

"It's true that we've left the best for last," the auctioneer was saying, making her tingle with pleasure. The hum of conversation in the audience made Sabrina wild with curiosity, but she didn't have the nerve to turn around and listen to what they were saying about her and her work. Zeebo patted her arm reassuringly, and Colin sat up in his chair.

"*Lady in Flight*," the auctioneer announced. "The artist is Sabrina Melendey. This work was brought to our attention by Mr. Arthur Wellington III, and reviewed by Maxwell Sinclair of *Art World*, who wrote, and I quote: 'A new evocation of the essence of motion has been defined by a new and captivating talent.' "

Sabrina could scarcely listen to her own bio as the man's voice continued. The moments ticked away in her head as she came closer and closer to the bittersweet thrill of seeing her work up for bid. The auctioneer began at last.

"The bidding will start at five thousand dollars. Five thousand, do I hear six?" A single second that seemed like an eternity passed, and then, "Six, do I hear—yes, seven?" He barely had to finish his calls before they were met. "Seven, eight, thank you, do I hear nine . . . nine . . ." Another infinite second passed. "Ten thousand, do I hear eleven?"

Now that it was actually happening, it was going too fast for her to think.

"Twelve, thirteen thousand, I have thirteen thousand, let me hear fourteen . . ." There was another one of those horrible pauses. "Fourteen thousand. Do I hear fifteen? Fifteen thousand?" The next pause was even longer, and Sabrina's hands twisted anxiously in her lap. "Fourteen thousand, going once . . . going twice . . ." She held her breath and waited. Time seemed to have stopped and she was quite unaware that she was squeezing Zeebo's hand with all her might.

"Fifteen!" The familiar sound of Arthur Wellington's voice shattered the suspended moment, charging the bidding with new excitement. A hum went around the room as everyone realized that the bidding was far from over. Sabrina let out a shaky breath and opened her eyes. At that instant she realized that it was Colin's hand, not Zeebo's, that she had been holding, and she looked up at him in surprise. He smiled at her, a smile so warm and engaging that she managed to smile back a little. Her hand stayed laced with his as the auction continued.

"Fifteen," the auctioneer called out. "Do I hear sixteen?" In half a second he had it. "Sixteen, sixteen thousand. Do I hear seventeen?" But again, he barely had to ask. Seventeen, eighteen, and nineteen all flew by, and within less than a minute, he was asking for twenty thousand dollars. Sabrina was trembling now, and she gripped Colin's hand almost convulsively.

"Do I hear twenty?" the auctioneer asked. He looked directly at Arthur Wellington, who nodded affirmatively. "Twenty thousand, do I hear twenty-one?"

Sabrina could hardly stand it. "My God," she whispered to herself. "Twice as much as I expected!"

"But only half what it's worth," Zeebo added self-righteously.

"Twenty thousand!" the auctioneer boomed. "The highest bid today." He paused dramatically, letting the fervor in the room increase. "Going once . . .

going twice . . ." The gavel started to come down, but at the last moment, he called. "Twenty-one!"

"Twenty-two," Arthur Wellington persisted.

The auctioneer saw another bid. "Twenty-three," he announced. Sabrina wondered frantically who was bidding against Wellington, but there were no clues.

Not to be outdone, Wellington again topped the bid. "Twenty-four," he called out.

"Who's the other bidder?" Sabrina couldn't help whispering to Zeebo. He gave her a knowing smile and jerked his thumb in Colin's direction. Incredulous, Sabrina turned to Colin in time to see him raise one finger.

"Twenty-five," came the response from the podium.

"Oh, no!" Sabrina cried, stunned. "Don't you dare!"

"Why not?" he answered casually, speaking in a low voice. "It's a free auction. I've always wanted to own a Melendey original."

Her eyes were blazing. "Since when?" she hissed.

"Twenty-six," Wellington chimed.

Colin's finger went up immediately, and this time his voice accompanied it. "Twenty-seven," he said in a clear, firm voice. Turning to Sabrina, he added quietly, "Since the other night, of course. You may not believe this, but I'm doing you a big favor by buying your sculpture. You're very lucky I came along when I did."

"*What?*" She wanted to strangle him.

"Twenty-eight!"

"Twenty-nine!" Colin countered swiftly.

"Thirty!" Wellington was just as determined as Colin, and the room was electric with the tension.

Frantic, Sabrina turned to Zeebo. "Stop him," she pleaded. "Do something!"

Zeebo looked at her in amazement. "Stop him?

How?" He thought for a moment. "And why should I?

"Thirty-one!" Colin was saying confidently.

"Thirty-two!" Wellington stayed in the running, and the hush in the room was filled with anticipation.

The auctioneer waited dramatically before taking up the reins. "I have thirty-two," he said smoothly. "Do I hear thirty-three?"

"Oh, what the heck," Colin said suddenly. He stood up with a decisive air and announced. "Thirty-five thousand. And well worth it."

For a long moment no one spoke. Even the auctioneer was speechless. Then he cleared his throat and turned to Wellington. "Sir?"

Wellington stood up and gestured deferentially toward Colin. "My congratulations," he said politely, "on a fine purchase."

The tension broke amid the loud, excited chatter of the audience and the gavel banged several times. "Sold!" the auctioneer declared triumphantly. "For thirty-five thousand dollars!"

The applause was boisterous as the photographers immediately surrounded Colin and Sabrina. Cameras clicked, bulbs flashed, and reporters swarmed, but Sabrina was too stunned to know how to react. Colin was chatting merrily with a reporter, but he saw the quandry she was in, and his strong arm went around her, holding her tightly against him. This was not necessarily what she wanted right now—not at all—but she stood there limply, not knowing whether to laugh or cry.

A reporter wearing a tailored suit with a fur collar, and a fancy hat, readied her pencil over her pad and turned to Sabrina. "I'm Gloria Johannson, from *Art International*," she said smoothly. "Is it true, Ms. Melendey, that you've never allowed any of your paintings to be sold?"

"I—what was that?" Sabrina was too dazed to hear

the question properly. She was conscious of nothing certain except the strong, anchoring arm holding her.

"Your paintings," the woman pressed. "Is it true that you've refused to sell them?"

"Not true at all!" It was Zeebo, shoving through a nearby group to reach her side. He approached the reporter and addressed her with an authoritative air. "It so happens that I just purchased three landscapes from Ms. Melendey." He tugged gently at Sabrina's elbow, and she tried to edge away from Colin, who was staring at Zeebo suspiciously.

"But," the reporter persisted, "do you feel that *Lady in Flight* is really worth thirty-five thousand dollars?" The question was pushy, but it was in the back of everyone's mind. Sabrina felt queasy as she waited for Zeebo's reply.

Zeebo smiled enigmatically and then shrugged. "It is now," he said with a wry shake of his head. "It is now."

He left the woman standing there as he pried Sabrina loose and led her away. She felt like a mechanical doll as he steadied her, and his friendly face was like a beacon in a sea of confusion.

"Oh, Zeebo!" she wailed. "What just happened?"

"Are you all right, Sabrina?" he asked with concern.

She took a deep breath and let it out slowly. "I don't know," she answered slowly. "I almost feel like a thief. This sure wasn't what I expected."

He chuckled, relishing the irony of it. "I know. But what you expected is irrelevant. It seems your friend Mr. Forrester has just established the going rate for your work." Without another word, he whipped out a checkbook and began to write out a check. "I'll be by tomorrow to pick up my paintings," he said casually. "In the meantime, I suggest that you start cataloguing all of your past work. I have a distinct feeling that it will be in demand by the end of the week." He ripped the check from the book and handed it to her with a flourish. "Here you are, Sabrina. I'm true to my word. I said I'd pay the going rate for your paintings, and I have." He smiled with satisfaction. "At last I am the owner of a Melendey original. Three, to be exact."

Sabrina glanced at the check and did a double take. The check was for the amount of $105,000. "What—what's this for?" she gasped.

"Those three paintings you did last summer. I just bought them. At last," he added as an afterthought. After kissing her on the cheek, he made his way over to the entrance and disappeared, leaving her all alone with her shock. She looked down again at the amount of the check, forcing herself to read it, but she couldn't seem to feel anything except numbness. The photographers saw her standing there and surrounded her, flashing their cameras in her glazed face.

Suddenly, she was facing people she had never known, people who were pressing forward to congratulate her. Their words of appreciation and admiration sounded sincere, but she simply couldn't believe what had just happened. It felt too easy. And too crazy. She listened speechlessly as the well-wishers expressed their interest in her, trying desperately to replay the auction in her mind and finding that she could barely remember it. It had all gone by so fast. She knew only that it had changed her life—and she wasn't sure she was ready for this kind of change.

"Let's have lunch next week," a woman in a purple turban was braying. "Here's my card. My gallery is on Madison and Fifty-seventh Street."

"I've always been a fan of yours," gushed a gentleman. Sabrina gulped. She had never seen the man before in her life. How could he be familiar with her work? She almost blushed when she realized that his band-wagon flattery had no basis in reality.

"A dinner for new artists at the Waldorf," the art gallery owner broke in. "You simply must come . . ."

Someone else was waving a pamphlet in front of her nose. ". . . a showing of Peruvian films. We'd love for you to attend."

"Sabrina!" A blessedly familiar voice broke the spell, and she looked up gratefully at Arthur Wellington, who was coming toward her.

"Oh, Mr. Wellington!" she cried.

"I'm proud of you, Sabrina," he said warmly. "Unfortunately, I lost out on a great work of art as well as the best window designer in town."

"Window designer . . ." she repeated blankly. Oh, yes. The Lloyd's windows. A welcome bit of reality at the moment. "Don't worry, Arthur," she smiled. "I'll take care of them. I won't break my commitment. In fact, I'll go down there this afternoon. I think I could use the break."

"Good, good," he said jovially. "And I'd like to talk to you about the still life that's hanging on your wall. I'm sure we can come to terms." He winked confidentially and moved off.

The flurry of reporters and curiosity-seekers gradually diminished, and Sabrina was able to work her way over to the door. She stood in front of two large windows that faced the street, and as she gazed down at the sidewalk, she saw *Lady in Flight* being wheeled out and loaded onto a truck. Somehow, this tangible proof that her sculpture had just sold for an astronomical sum and was now traveling permanently out of her life made her weak with emotion. Tears blinded her eyes and bright spots of color sprang to her cheeks as she watched her beloved work carted off like a piece of furniture. And the worst part was that it was not going to the home of an appreciative patron or a discerning collector. It was going off to be mercilessly scrutinized, poked at, and possibly even dissected! And at the Museum of Natural History, of all places!

Sabrina closed her eyes for a moment, bitterly remembering the dream that she, like all young artists, had always cherished: the exhibition of her work at the Museum of Modern Art. She had imagined the glory, the overwhelming sense of achievement. Her heart had quickened at the thought that maybe, just maybe, she could be one of the truly talented. And now? A humorless laugh escaped her throat. Well, now her work would be in a museum, all right. The wrong one.

Feeling completely defeated, she blinked back the tears and turned to leave. The last person in the world she wanted to see right now was Colin, but there he was, listening with interest to a reporter's questions. He looked up and saw her standing there alone, and suddenly she was filled with a rush of anger. Her eyes blazed green fire as she stared at him pointedly, not letting him look away. Had she been feeling sorry for herself just a moment ago? *Why?* She had done nothing wrong. And she was still Sabrina Melendey, the creator of *Lady in Flight*, the most exciting new sculpture of the year. She wouldn't let him make a mockery of her work! She couldn't! She hadn't struggled for all those years just to see all of her efforts wasted. Even for thirty-five thousand dollars. She knew now that the money wasn't enough. She was an artist, not a banker.

The reporter's voice faded into the background as Colin caught Sabrina's fiery stare. His sharp eyes caressed her lovely face, seeing her vulnerability and her courage, and he knew exactly what she was thinking. He read her mind effortlessly, feeling her anger as tangibly as shock waves from across the room. She almost trembled with the force of her conviction, and he wanted to rush over and take her in his arms.

No! he wanted to shout. I'm not going to destroy your work! Don't you know that I could never do that, not after seeing inside your soul as clearly as I do now? His stance tightened, making the long lines of his body hard and uncompromising as he stared back at her. The current between them was almost palpable. Breaking abruptly away from the reporter, Colin strode across the room toward Sabrina.

She saw him coming and suddenly panicked. She didn't want to face him, not yet. Not until she had a plan of some kind. She already knew how persuasive he could be, and a deeply buried part of her didn't want to admit how much he had already affected her. If she let him touch her, even once . . .

Sabrina turned and fled from the room, darting out to the elevator and uttering a hasty, silent prayer of thanks that was open and empty. She dashed inside, pressed a button, and breathed a loud sigh of relief when the doors banged shut just as Colin rounded the corner in search of her. When she reached the ground floor, she exited cautiously, expecting to see him rushing out of the stairwell, but no one was there. She slipped outside and started walking up Madison Avenue, her feet pounding the concrete.

Colin had stopped short at the elevator, respecting her obvious wish to be alone. He would talk to her later. Now that she was gone, he walked back slowly into the auction room, mumbling an apology to the reporter and keeping one eye still cocked toward the door in the hope that she would return. The vision of her pale, beautiful face still hung in his mind as if her ghost were hovering over him.

He resignedly turned his full attention to the reporter and listened to him once again.

"But why were you so fervent about owning *Lady*

in *Flight?*" the man asked. "Was it the artist's ability to capture the feeling of movement?"

Movement. Flight. Sabrina was in flight right now. "Yes," Colin answered slowly. "Yes, that's it. That feeling of inexpressible grace, of fluid, feminine movement . . ."

The reporter hastily jotted all of this down.

"She's like an incorrigible angel with a totally free spirit," Colin continued, almost to himself.

"And you feel that this trend is unusual?"

"Unusual?" Colin's mouth curved unconsciously in a wistful smile. "I would say unique." A vision of Sabrina floated through his mind. "And the best thing that's happened to me since . . . since Godzilla destroyed Cleveland." He punctuated this odd remark with a private little laugh, leaving the reporter to haplessly record his unorthodox remarks.

Sabrina spent the next two hours wandering the streets, trying to bring herself down to earth. It didn't do any good. She remained dazed as she walked through the park, oblivious to the afternoon bicycle riders and roller skaters, emerging on the West Side with her mind still in a jumble. She was standing on Central Park West at Eighty-first Street, and the large and familiar bulk of the Museum of Natural History loomed directly in front of her. Chuckling ruefully to herself, she realized that she still had a job to do there. She had promised Arthur Wellington she would get to it today.

Now seemed as good a time as any, so she walked over to the side entrance she had used with Colin and rang the bell. A guard came, checked her identification, and let her in, escorting her over to the warehouse where the items to be sent over to Lloyd's were being held. A short, bespectacled man greeted her and told her to double-check each item, tagging each one with her initials if she was satisfied.

This was exactly the kind of task she needed, she

reflected with pleasurable relief. It was methodical, routine, and calming. She went to work quickly, going through crates and insurance forms, noting which items would make the trip over to Lloyd's and which ones would be sent back to storage. She worked for the better part of an hour, checking and initialing, tagging and inspecting, until at last she came upon a crate that looked as if it had just been delivered.

There was something strangely familiar about this crate, and although it was not marked as one of the Lloyd's items, she looked inside curiously. The box was about her height, and as she peered inside, she saw something that made her jump. Right in front of her eyes, visible through the slats, was the backside of *Lady in Flight*, still distinguished by the five protrusions. They must have brought it over just before I arrived, she thought hastily. Her marking pen hovered for only a moment as she looked around furtively. No one was watching her. The bespectacled man sat placidly reading a detective novel, and the large, musty room was quiet. Then she quickly scrawled her initials on the tag, clearly indicating that the crate should be sent over to Lloyd's Fifth Avenue along with the other items.

Twenty minutes later, she was finished with the inventory. She signed out, thanked the guards, and hung around outside while the truck was being loaded, trying to look casual. When *Lady in Flight* was hoisted up and placed inside the large delivery truck, she breathed a triumphant sigh of relief and left, feeling as if she had just been handed a priceless second chance.

Chapter Five

" 'Who's a primate?' " Sabrina read aloud from the large banner that waved in front of the museum. The banner was advertising a new exhibit that depicted the evolution of man.

"I am," said a cheerful voice behind her. "And so are you."

She wheeled and saw Colin standing there, his arms folded across his chest. "What—what did you do?" she said, gaping. "Follow me here?"

"Not exactly," he answered mildly, his candid eyes boring into her. "I do work here, you know."

"Oh. Well, I was just leaving." She started to back away, but he reached out and took her arm.

"Wait, Sabrina," he said gently. "Don't leave." Her eyes flashed suspiciously. "We have to talk."

"There's nothing to talk about," she announced firmly.

"Oh, but there is." His hand tightened its grip on her arm, forcing her to stay where she was. "Have dinner with me."

"Let go of me," she commanded. "Your brute force isn't exactly persuasive."

He laughed and let go. "All right. Then let's talk sensibly. I have a lot to tell you, and I'm not really in the mood to work tonight. If you leave, I'll have no excuse not to."

A tiny frown crossed her features as she realized that his work would probably involve the piece of sculpture he had just purchased. If he went into the museum now, he would discover that it was missing. . . .

"Oh, all right," she said, deepening her frown. "If you insist."

"I do," he said, brightening. "As one primate to another, I promise you won't be sorry." She couldn't help laughing, and he hailed a cab and opened the door. "After you, madam."

At Colin's direction, the taxi sped down to Sixty-fifth Street, depositing them in front of a large town-house.

"Where are we?" Sabrina asked, still suspicious.

"We're just going to stop at my place for a minute." He dug in his pocket for his keys and led her up the steps.

Colin lived on the parlor floor in a large apartment that had windows facing both the street and the garden. Sabrina expected it to look like an army barracks—rigid, colorless, and neat as a pin. But when she stepped inside, she saw that every inch of it was put to some kind of use. The living room held comfortable, roomy furniture that looked invitingly lived-in, and part of it seemed to be used as an impromptu office. A large, office-sized desk with a red tonsure lamp clamped onto the side sat in one corner, and she saw that it was piled high with books and papers. Bamboo shades covered the windows, and a few hanging plants basked in the light in front of them. It should have looked cluttered, but somehow it only looked very busy, as if its occupant was always involved in some new project.

There was only one thing that seemed lacking. Sabrina, as a matter of habit, always looked at people's walls when she first entered their apartments to see what dominated their taste in art. Most people had a few prints or photographs, and her eye would naturally stray to see what their choices would reveal about them.

But Colin didn't have anything that could be called art. Or, if he did, it wasn't put out in the open—probably because there wasn't any room. The walls were lined with shelves, and the shelves were filled, row upon row, with books of every size and shape. Sabrina had never seen so many books together in one place, except in a library.

"My God," was the first thing she said after looking around. "Have you actually read all of these books?"

Colin looked surprised, but he nodded. "Most of them. Why?"

She didn't answer. She was busy perusing the many titles, smiling as she came across a large volume called *The Cave Paintings of Early Man*. Most of the books seemed scientifically oriented, but there were many novels and works about literature as well, along with a variety of other subjects. Sabrina had always thought that a room without artistic influence or design would be empty and spiritless, but this room seemed to brim with life. The books provided color and warmth of their own, many of them like old, old friends. Her eye stopped at a shelf of children's books.

"*Tom Swift?*" she said teasingly. "One of your reference books?"

"In a way," he answered seriously. "It was books like that that first got me interested in science." He came up behind her and placed his hands on her shoulders. "Sabrina, listen—"

She spun around to face him. "It's too late," she stated bluntly. "It's all over."

"Nothing is over. You had the success you wanted today, didn't you?" His hands remained on her shoulders and there was a glint in his eye.

"Is that your idea of success?" she cried, her anger

and resentment returning in a rush. "You made a mockery of everything I've been working toward."

His hands dropped, but he didn't move away. "That's not true," he said flatly. "I drove the price of it much higher than you ever expected it to go."

"But for all the wrong reasons!" she flared, her eyes brimming suddenly with tears. "You bought a specimen, not a work of art!"

"So what? No one knows that except you and me." He stepped forward, narrowing the already narrow space between them until she was backed up against the bookshelves.

"But—but you're going to destroy it!" she cried. "My best work, right down the drain . . ." Now that the first tears had slipped out, Sabrina couldn't control the rest. They slid helplessly down her face, forming two wet lines of anguish that only seemed to make him more fierce and determined than he already was.

"All right, Sabrina," he said grimly. "Since you're so positive that I'm an ogre, I'll make a deal with you."

She eyed him warily. "What kind of deal?"

"I won't do anything to that statue that you wouldn't do . . . on two conditions." He waited, and she considered, frowning.

"Which are?"

"Which are that you agree to show me the site where you found that piece of limestone, and I mean the exact spot. And—" His face softened a little. "And you agree to have dinner with me."

"That's all?" She sniffed suspiciously.

He smiled gently. "That's all."

"Well . . ." She looked down at the floor, wondering if she could trust him, and realizing that she didn't have a choice. She stiffened slightly as she felt his hands touch her shoulders again, and she was suddenly filled with an unbearable longing. Two more tears ran down her cheeks as she wished desperately for an answer. "I feel so alone," she whispered, almost against her will.

His arms moved around her when she said that, enclosing her protectively. "You're anything but alone, Sabrina," he whispered back, holding her very close. "I swear, I won't do anything to harm your work. Don't you think I have any sensitivity at all? Can't you see how I'm beginning to feel about you?"

She looked up, her tear-streaked face an open book that he read easily. He knew that she still had doubts about him, but that she didn't want to have those doubts. She wanted more, much more.

Sabrina searched his face and decided to gamble. It wasn't just that she had no choice. It was that she needed to believe in him. And the look in his eyes sent a shiver through her that had the force of lightning.

The tiny space between them closed as his mouth met hers. Colin was deliberately gentle at first, holding himself in check, but his need for her was so strong that she felt the currents of it penetrating her last layer of defense. This, she told herself in a rush of honesty, was what she had been avoiding so strenuously. Sabrina had known, deep down, what would happen to her as soon as she surrendered to his touch. His mouth teased her and probed her, still gentle but very insistent, awakening her own desire almost effortlessly. She would almost have been embarrassed at how very easily he could arouse her, except that she knew he was reacting just as swiftly to the magic as she was.

She clung to him, her hands touching the rippling muscles of his back, and it was she who found his tongue with her own and began the sinuous dance that seemed to shut out the rest of the world. The kiss deepened and became more feverish. When at last it broke, he followed it up with tiny kisses that rained on her face, her hair, and her throat. All of Sabrina's doubt vanished at this tender onslaught. She was seized with a sudden joy, and she actually smiled as she let her head fall back, reveling in the feel of his hands luxuriating in her long, silky hair.

Colin stopped and looked down at her, his eyes shining a deep blue. A shock of hair had fallen across his forehead, and his face, usually sparkling with keen intelligence, was now lined with desire.

"Please," she whispered, her eyes half closed. "Please."

"I will," he vowed, gathering her close again. His fingertips began a tormenting dance up and down her slender frame, savoring the curve of her hips and pausing to linger on her small breasts. They responded instantly, rising to fullness even before he grasped them in his eager hands, and a moan of longing escaped her.

"Come," he said raggedly, taking her hand. She followed him down the hall to a bedroom that was also lined with books, but this time she didn't stop to look. She sat on the edge of the bed and let him undress her, her clothes falling away easily as each part of her body was revealed to his hungry eyes. When he unclasped the lacy white bra and slowly drew it away to expose her breasts, he stared at them with undisguised need.

Sabrina took his hands and placed them on her breasts, giving them a gentle squeeze, and he groaned with desire, anchoring his body on the bed by placing a knee on either side of her hips. His mouth quickly followed his hands, tasting the sweetness of each rosy nipple, and his nose buried itself in the firm, round fullnesses that surrounded each one. Sabrina was lost in a world of sensual awareness, feeling and knowing nothing except the need to possess him. Her body climbed the spiral he created, rising to higher and higher peaks until her breath was

hoarse and out of control. His tongue traced a delicate pattern down her torso and over the gentle swell
of her stomach. She was now lying back on the bed,
but her legs hung over the edge, imprisoned by his
knees. When he slipped down to the floor, pushing
her thighs apart with his hands, she cried out in delicious anticipation. He teased the insides of her
thighs, first with delicate fingers and then with the
warmth of his mouth, leaving a trail of fire that made
her arch beneath him. Her legs opened wider of their
own accord, inviting him to taste her inner sweetness, and he teased her, darting back and forth from
one satiny thigh to the other, deliberately ignoring
her breathless need. But at last he obliged her, center-
ing on her very core with tiny, feathery strokes that
sent her hurtling into another world. His strong
hands held her hips as he sent arrows of fire through
her blood.

Sabrina's whole body flushed with pleasure, and
she felt herself being pulled closer and closer to complete abandon. She tried feebly to stop him, afraid
that she would be spent before she could please him,
but he only continued to intensify his butterfly
strokes. At last her hips arched, out of control, as
great tidal waves shook her body, and she cried out
her passion in total surrender.

A minute passed as she lay there, limp and trembling, and then his hands began another sensuous
journey up her thighs and over her hips to find the
firm softness of her breasts. She was amazed at how
quickly she could respond to him again. She was still
deeply sensitive from the culmination that had just
passed, but Colin went slowly, coaxing another flood
of desire to well up within her.

This time she was more aggressive, wanting to give
him as much pleasure as he had given her. She sat up
and pulled him onto the bed, gently unbuttoning his
shirt and slowly removing it before reaching for the

rest of his clothes. She removed them carefully, watching his eyes as she did so, and raking her nails down the length of his sinewy chest.

"Oh, Sabrina," he murmured, casting a long, slow glance over her small frame. "Just stay still long enough for me to drive you insane."

Her eyes glowed emerald in the shadows. "You already have," she whispered. Leaning over him, she kissed him gently several times and ran her hands over the smooth, hard lines of his body. They fell back together, Sabrina still placing small, firm kisses on his shoulders and his chest as her hand dipped to tease his masculinity. The moment she touched him, he shuddered uncontrollably and let out a soft, harsh cry of masculine need. She moved very slowly, with soft, almost weightless touches, causing him to close his eyes and revel under her deft hand.

"Shall I drive you insane now?" she asked softly, slipping down on the bed to add her tongue to the maddening caresses. As her mouth slowly savored him, her hands found the hard, lean muscles of his thighs, and she was surprised at how much the feel of him beneath her fingers aroused her. Her pace became feverish as she found herself responding urgently, wanting to torment him but wanting to lose herself as well.

Then, as if he had read the movements of her body, he flipped over and pinned her underneath, positioning his knees between her soft thighs. Her body opened to him readily, drinking him in with undisguised hunger. Now he was in control again, moving with a slow, sensual rhythm inside of her. Sabrina felt the inside of her body tingle and then close around him. The electricity coursed down her legs and into her toes, and his weight crushed her breasts against him. Somehow she wanted to be as absolutely close to him at this moment as she could possibly be, and she whispered, "Please hold me," into his ear.

Colin responded instantly, sliding his strong arms under her back to hold her tightly. After a moment he kept one arm under her shoulders and moved the other one down under her hips to guide her as they moved together and apart, together and apart.

Sabrina was no longer sure who was driving whom insane, and she didn't care. They were riding a current that floated magnetically between them, each needing the other in order to continue the passionate spiral they had created. She felt that she could lie here like this with him forever, relishing the sweet, savory sensation of his body exploring hers.

"How well we fit together," he murmured, his eyes closed.

She could not answer him, but reflected that it was true. She felt lush and beautiful, receiving him with graceful ease. He held her hips tightly against him and penetrated her even more deeply, causing her to gasp in pleasure. She felt filled now, complete. They rocked together with a new rhythm, feeling so utterly lost in each other that they lost rhythm altogether and crashed against each other with driving force. Sabrina felt his hardness break as her body collapsed upon itself, sending waves of release through every muscle and nerve ending. She fell back, exhilarated but spent.

Colin was lying on her, his face buried in her shoulder, and it was a long time before either one of them spoke. At last he lifted his head and moved his body so that he was lying next to her, his leg aligned with hers. They opened their eyes and looked at each other.

"Hi," Sabrina said gently.

He smiled, his eyes caressing her bare body. "Hi."

That was all for awhile, but there was no need for further words. They had all the communication they needed in the little smiles, the gentle caresses, and the tiny sighs of contentment that filled the room for the next several minutes.

Then Sabrina sat up, looking around for a clock. She didn't find one, but her eyes took in the rows of books and stopped suddenly at one shelf that looked startlingly familiar.

"Hey," she said pleasantly.

"What is it?"

"I see you have a whole collection of the Jack Ames series," she noted. The boys' adventure books were all original editions, obviously kept from childhood.

"Yeah." He smiled lazily. "I still have every one. I could never get rid of them. They're too much a part of me."

Sabrina smiled. "I know what you mean. I read every one."

"You did?" He ran a finger down her back. "I didn't know girls read adventure books."

"I read these," she countered. "Because my father wrote them."

He sat up next to her, clearly surprised. "He did?" he asked, looking at her with new respect. "Well, that's really something." He draped his arm around her bare shoulders and chuckled. "I guess we have more in common than I thought."

Chapter Six

❧

The chic and glittering main floor of Lloyd's Fifth Avenue looked very, very odd the next morning. Perched at odd angles in between the cosmetics counters were various models of skeletons from the Museum of Natural History. And running frantically to and fro in the midst of the whole thing were the designers. Sabrina was among them, looking slightly frazzled as she tried to find what she needed for the window. She was certainly not used to being up at this hour of the morning. It was only seven-thirty, and she usually didn't get up before noon. Neither, she guessed from their appearance, did the other designers. But it was necessary to have the windows begun and the exhibits arranged before the hordes of shoppers arrived, especially when the displays were as delicate and unusual as these.

When her group of models appeared, Sabrina worked quickly but carefully, checking the tag on each item and directing its transport, and gradually the chaos began to take shape. Climbing in and out of the store windows and constantly checking her clipboard, she slowly orchestrated the procedure. It would actually take several days to get everything into final position, but by the middle of that first morning, the worst of the confusion was under control. There was one tense moment when one of the more complex models slipped, careening perilously to one side, but the workers uprighted it without mishap. As the various items found their assigned places, Sabrina was faced with the problem of what to do with one particular piece that looked decidedly out of place.

Alone and beautiful, *Lady in Flight* stood in all its splendor near the entrance, waiting patiently to be moved. Sabrina decided that perhaps she should send it back to the museum after all, and was about to tell the workmen to put the crate back into the truck, when Arthur Wellington ambled by. She didn't want him to know that *Lady in Flight* was sitting in the middle of his store, so she reached for a nearby rack of dresses and slipped one off its hanger. Wellington didn't see her as she hastily pulled the flowery silk over the statue's head and smoothed it into place, smirking at the odd results. *Lady in Flight* was now clothed in the very latest designer sportswear.

"Not bad," she observed with a critical eye, "but it needs a hat." She dashed over to the hat department and picked a straw one with a wide brim. Then she picked up a pair of sunglasses and a scarf and ran back. The accessories disguised the sculpture surprisingly well, and after a moment's scrutiny, Sabrina filched a tennis raquet from another mannequin and stuck it into the crook of the *Lady's* arm. She directed one of the workers to place the odd figure in the front center window, where it was deposited next to a Neanderthal man and the rudiments of a campfire. Sabrina climbed into the window to survey the results, and her smile of satisfaction was accompanied by a distinct sigh of relief.

"Phew," she said aloud. "That was a close call."

"What was?" A strong arm encircled her waist and pulled her close for a moment as Colin planted a kiss on the side of her neck.

"Colin!" she exclaimed in surprise, instinctively backing away. "What are you doing here?"

"Hey, what's the matter?" he asked. "That's no

way to treat a guy who spent the night making passionate—"

"Shhh!" Sabrina didn't want any of the workers or Arthur Wellington to overhear any intimate conversations, and she didn't want Colin to see her statue. *His* statue. But her eyes softened a little as they roamed over his face, and she offered a tentative smile.

"That's better," he pronounced. "I came to say good-bye. I have to fly up to Ontario today, but I'll be back by tomorrow. You left so wretchedly early this morning that I didn't get a chance to tell you how much I enjoyed the evening." His voice was velvety, and he took a step forward.

"I enjoyed it too," she said quietly. A deep, full silence followed as they stared at each other, taking each other in again.

"You know," he said, gently breaking the spell, "you still owe me one of the two conditions you agreed to yesterday."

Her eyes twinkled. "Oh?"

"That's right. You're supposed to show me the exact spot where you found that stone."

Her cheeks burned a little as she realized that he was standing only a few feet away from the stone in question, but she only said, "That's no problem. I'm only wondering if I've really fulfilled the other condition—the one to have dinner. I'm not sure that ordering a pizza and eating it in bed after hours and hours of feverish lovemaking qualifies as dinner."

"I see," he grinned. "Perhaps we'll arrange a raincheck. But I'm afraid that finding another fossil just like the one in your statue is going to be something of a problem." She frowned. "It takes more than two people to go fossil hunting," he explained. "It's actually a very painstaking process, like a detective hunt. Usually hundreds of people are employed for a search like this. I spent the morning on the phone trying to round up a party of students, but I couldn't get enough people together at the last minute without advance notice."

Sabrina nodded slowly, but then she was hit with an idea. "I've got the perfect solution," she said suddenly.

He looked doubtful, and she continued eagerly.

"The answer is simple," she said. "The Mangia Society."

"The *what?*"

"You remember. The Mangia Society. My friend Allegra is the president. There are hundreds of members and we all meet once a month to share some kind of extravagant food experience." Her eyes sparkled merrily, as if the problem were now solved.

"So?" he persisted. "What does that have to do with fossil hunting?"

"We'll invite the Mangia Society on a picnic in the Adirondacks," she explained. "Then we'll split up into groups and you can tell everyone what to look for."

Colin brightened immediately. "Will they go for that?"

"Sure," she shrugged. "Why not? We've done crazier things, believe me."

"That's great, Sabrina!" he said enthusiastically. "But I'll have to prepare maps, get photos, organize the group in relays—and I have to go to Ontario first! I don't know if I can—"

"Whoa!" she said, laughing. "Relax. You can do all of that later—after we arrive in the Adirondacks. No one in the Mangia Society is going to go just to look for a bunch of fossils. They're mainly interested in the food." Her eyes gleamed. "And Allegra and I will take care of that."

Colin still looked hopeful, but a shadow of doubt crossed his face. "You're not going to leave it all to the last minute?"

Her laughter trilled around them, and she placed a reassuring hand on his arm. "Leave everything to me. By the time we get back, you'll feel like you've been upstate with the Hardy boys."

He laughed and she looked up at him coyly. "You know," she said, "I think you're beginning to appreciate me."

"Oh, I appreciate you," he said in a low voice, stepping forward to put his arms around her. Sabrina took a step backwards, conscious that they were standing in the window of a large department store on Fifth Avenue, but Colin didn't care. He leaned one elbow casually on the nearest mannequin, which happened to be *Lady in Flight*, and looked down into Sabrina's eyes. "I'll miss you tonight," he added, stroking her arms. "But we'll make up for it when I get back."

She stared at him solemnly, feeling the sweetly familiar rush spreading to her fingertips. His face was vulnerable and open, reflecting his desire, and she wondered what really went on in his mind, what it was that really made him tick. She knew that he was quirky and single-minded and even brilliant at times, and she knew that a raw passion smoldered beneath his inquisitive exterior. He was unlike any man she had ever known. There was no logical reason why she should be attracted to him, but she knew now that all he had to do was touch her and she would unravel under his hands. Colin could make her want him fiercely just by lightly stroking her arms, as he was doing now.

"Colin . . ." she whispered, trying desperately to fight the sensation even as she prayed for him to continue.

"Good-bye, Elf," he whispered back, doing nothing to conceal the longing he felt.

She managed to smile a little. "Elf?"

His hands strayed to her waist, where they sensuously molded her feminine curves, only inches from the slopes of her breasts. "Oh, that's my new name for you—Elf. Come here."

He pulled her close, holding her by the hips. Then she was crushed against him as he kissed her, seeking her tongue immediately and caressing it with his own in long, relishing strokes. His stance was firm and commanding—legs apart, narrow hips thrust forward—and she melted against him, her own legs beginning to tremble.

The kiss was long and provocative, and he followed it up at once with another one and then another one that sent her senses spinning. Vaguely she thought that they should stop standing there and lie down on a bed or even slip to the floor, but then she remembered weakly that there was no bed, and she did not have the strength to lift her mouth from his. Suddenly he trembled violently, and she was shaken with a bolt of desire that was rooted in the realization of how much she was arousing him.

He pressed her close, wanting to possess all of her. "God, woman, what you do to me," he whispered savagely into her hair. "I can't have enough of you."

His words made her eyes blink open, and she remembered in a rush of embarrassment where they were. "Colin!" she said urgently, trying to still his advances but not wanting to shove him away. "Stop!"

He knew what she meant, but he didn't care. "Never mind that," he returned fiercely. "This is New York. No one will look. Kiss me good-bye."

"I did," she said lamely, but he kissed her again.

Sabrina's eye caught the stare of a woman who was passing the window, and she became frantic. "Colin! I mean it! Let go of me!" The woman was joined by two teenagers who stopped abruptly to ogle them, and a moment later a man with a briefcase joined the audience.

Colin only kissed her again and continued to hold her in his warm embrace. Sabrina saw through her extreme discomfort that the small group of onlookers was watching with curious amusement, and their interested stares caught the attention of even more passersby.

"Colin!" she shouted, losing all sense of decorum. "Stop it! We've got an audience, for heaven's sake!"

He stopped so suddenly, with such perfect precision, that she knew all at once that he had been teasing her. Turning ceremoniously to the people outside, he gave them a gallant bow, holding the pose for a long moment before straightening up again.

Sabrina stared at him, flushed and angry, and he burst out laughing when he saw the furious look on her face. The impromptu audience all laughed too, some of them applauding cheerfully, and Sabrina looked wildly back and forth between Colin and the group. A wicked grin spread across her face as her sense of humor took charge, and Colin's face dropped as she grabbed the club from the hand of the inert Neanderthal that stood next to them and brandished it above her head. Colin moved away precipitately, almost backing into the well-dressed figure of *Lady in Flight*.

"Watch out!" she called, following him menacingly, the club held over her head with both hands. She followed him slowly, right around the statue and over to the exit from the window, disappearing from public view.

Back inside the store, he turned and held her by the shoulders, his face suddenly serious. "Good-bye, Elf," he said, leaving a lingering kiss on her mouth. And with that, he turned and walked past the last of the dinosaurs, disappearing through the revolving doors.

Sabrina stared after him, shaking her head in defeat. But then she smiled. *Lady in Flight* had remained serenely safe, her secret intact.

Chapter Seven

❧

MANGIA SOCIETY BULLETIN

Our next outing will be a French provincial country picnic on Saturday, May 12th in the Adirondack Mountains. Those interested in offering or receiving a ride should contact Veronica Coyne, the carpool chairperson. Please plan to meet at 11:00 A.M. in front of the town hall in Northville, New York. Directions and the menu are enclosed.

Allegra Russo, President

Sabrina reflected peacefully on the previous week as she and Colin bounced along in his truck on the way up to the Adirondacks. The ride was long and soothing, and the quiet country air refreshed her spirits.

Oddly enough, it wasn't the money she had made or the success she had found that dominated her thoughts. Those things were wonderful, but after all her hard work she had expected them. No, it was the man sitting next to her whom she found herself thinking about, because he was the only thing that didn't make sense.

, He had entered her life unexpectedly, and not only had he irrevocably influenced her professional status, he had become a permanent fixture in her personal life as well. It had only been a week, and yet somehow, she felt as if she had known him much longer. But that wasn't what confused her. What bothered her was that Colin was unlike the sort of man she had always been attracted to, and the two of them seemed to have absolutely nothing in common. Yet she always felt at ease with him, ready to trust him with her thoughts. And all rationality was lost when he took her in his arms. The passion between them had not diminished in the past week; it had mushroomed. It was not unusual for them to spend hours at a time making love, completely losing track of the time. But even that seemed paradoxical. Sabrina had dropped by Colin's office one afternoon and had waited for him to finish a lengthy business conversation on the phone. He had been crisp, dry, and thoroughly professional. And the minute he had hung up the phone, he had removed his glasses, taken her in his arms, and kissed her with a depth of stimulation that had left her weak and craving more.

She admired his intelligence and his dedication to his work, even though it often seemed rather dreary. He seemed equally ignorant about her work, though. At least he had never said anything about it. She didn't even know if he liked the piece of work he had bought so unexpectedly. *Lady in Flight* sat in his office at the museum, thankfully transferred back there after he had left for Ontario, and so far he had been true to his word. He had measured, X-rayed, and diagrammed, but he hadn't actually changed Sabrina's piece of art. She sighed unconsciously. He was an enigma. A complete enigma.

He showed up at Lloyd's every day around noon, and they would have lunch together. She knew nothing about paleontology, and he knew next to nothing about art, but somehow they always found plenty to talk about. She discovered that he was full of surprises.

The biggest surprise had come just yesterday. They

had arranged to have lunch in Central Park opposite the museum, and she had planned an imaginative picnic. Dressed in a loose knit dress, she packed lobster salad, French bread, Italian celery, and cold cherry soup into a basket and ventured over to the museum. He had told her to meet him at the North American Indian exhibits.

Strolling into the museum at noon, she found the right area quickly, but discovered that it would take a few minutes for her eyes to adjust to the musky darkness. She could barely make out the silhouetted figures of a dozen or so schoolchildren listening to the quiet voice of an instructor . . . Colin? She tiptoed over and found that it wasn't Colin, but a teacher giving a tour. The man led his small charges away, and she found herself quite alone in the dark, silent hall.

Looking around uncertainly, her eye fell on the nearest display, which pictured a life-size scene of four Indians grouped around a campfire. One of them was roasting a rabbit on a spit over the flames, and another was just emerging from an open teepee that was decorated with simple designs.

"Colin!" she called into the darkness. "Are you here?"

"Be right with you."

She jumped. "Where are you?"

"Waiting for lunch to be served." She looked around wildly, but the voice seemed to be coming out of thin air. Then she started in shock when one of the Indians around the campfire smiled at her. "I hope you brought something tastier than this old rabbit," he said.

Sabrina found her voice. "I don't believe you," she sputtered. She looked him up and down. He was wearing a suede jacket that had blended confusingly with the other Indian garb, and his jeans had been camouflaged by the dim light. A full-feathered Indian headdress was perched on his head. "What

are you doing down here?" she continued in disbelief. "I thought your territory was upstairs."

He picked up a large bone and held it out for her to
see. "I'm burying an old bone."

"Looks more like you're burying the hatchet," she
quipped. "You scared the daylights out of me." Her
eyes took in the details of the display, and she
noticed other bones that were lying around. "Well, it
looks like an authentic Arizona scene," she concluded. "And you fit right in."

"Close," he smiled. "Try South Dakota."

"Oh. Well, you're not a bad window dresser," she
smiled back. "And I should know."

"What's on the menu for today?" He reached out
for the basket and she handed it to him.

"I brought cold cherry soup, lobster salad, French
bread, and—"

"Cold soup!"

"It's dessert," she explained. "It's got cherries,
sour cream, sugar, and nutmeg."

Colin sat back down in the exhibit. "Okay, let's
eat."

"In there?"

"Sure." He was opening the basket and taking out
the food. "I'm starved. Besides, I'm on a tight schedule. I have to finish down here by the weekend and
I'm already behind."

She looked around self-consciously and then
stepped over the small security fence around the
scene.

"Sit over here," he said, patting the ground next to
him. "It's not real dirt," he assured her. She settled
down next to him, and before she could protest he
had placed a feather in her hair and had dropped a
circle of beads around her neck. "There, now we
won't be disturbed," he said, pleased. "We fit right
in." He dished out some of the lobster salad and tore
off a piece of bread. Two camera-laden tourists

strolled by, looking at them curiously. "How does it feel to be on display?" he asked cheerfully. "Say, this is delicious," he added without waiting for a reply.

The tourists walked on to another display, and Sabrina shook her head ruefully. "It feels strange to be the object of curiosity. Usually I'm just the window dresser," she reminded him. "And I'm glad you like the lobster. But next week I'm taking you for sushi."

His face went sour. "Forget it."

"Oh, Colin," she protested. "Don't be a killjoy. Do you know what sushi is?"

He nodded vigorously. "Yeah. Raw fish. Like I said, forget it. I won't touch that stuff."

She was about to launch into a persuasive speech when a group of people came by. They all stared pointedly at Colin and Sabrina as they filed by, and she continued in a low voice. "You know, for a guy who's been on expeditions chasing dinosaurs," she said in a heated whisper, "you don't have a very good sense of adventure. I should think that if you could withstand being bitten by a tyrannosaurus rex, you could try one little bite of something as delicious as sushi."

Colin shook his head. "No way. I once had something similar when I was on an expedition in the Arctic Circle. My host's dining room was made of snow, and he went out to catch dinner by digging a hole in the ice in his front yard and spearing through it. I never knew what it was that he caught, but we ate it raw." His face soured as he remembered it. "It just about made me sick."

"I didn't know you were in the Arctic," she said with new respect.

He began to laugh. "It was a far cry from Cedar Grove, I can tell you that."

"Cedar Grove? Which expedition was that?"

"It wasn't. It's my hometown. Cedar Grove, Montana."

"Cedar Grove, Montana?" she repeated incredulously. "Where's that?"

He pointed a finger straight up in the air. "North," he answered. "Very north."

"I didn't know that," she said slowly. "New Yorkers aren't all that familiar with all those in-between states."

"So I gather," he said dryly.

"I can't get over it. And to think you tried to make fun of me because you thought I came from the all-American apple pie family. Hah! You're the one, not me."

"I wasn't trying to make fun of you," he said reasonably.

She was shaking her head. "Cedar Grove. Wow. I still can't believe it." He nodded calmly, unimpressed by her antics. "And don't tell me you went to Cedar Grove High," she pressed.

"As a matter of fact, I did," he beamed. "Captain of the football team. Swim meets, the 4-H club, and sock hops in the gym."

She was laughing in spite of herself. "Touché. And you went to Cedar Grove Community College, right?"

"Something like that," he deadpanned, "only it was a small state college."

"How midwestern!" She crunched into a piece of celery. "And then graduate school, right?"

"Of course."

She couldn't help laughing again. "At that state school, right?"

"Wrong." He put down the piece of bread he was holding and reached up to adjust his feathers. "Cambridge."

There was a small silence. "Cambridge, Massachusetts?" she asked finally.

"No," he sighed, "England." His eyes twinkled. "You really shouldn't be so naive, Sabrina."

She sat up, pretending to be offended. "Me? Naive?"

"Yes. People who don't come from New York aren't hillbillies, you know. Some of us can even read and write."

"Okay, okay. What did you do after that?"

"Oh, I traveled around a lot. The Arctic, Tibet, Mexico, Peru. Plus some places that I couldn't spell and could barely locate on a map." He smiled ironically. "Let me know if I start boring you. Sometimes my life sounds like a National Geographic catalogue."

"Don't be silly," she said, fascinated. "I can see now why you wanted to settle down here to a desk job."

"Desk job!" He laughed loudly, but stopped short when his eyes made contact with a little boy who had sidled up to the exhibit and was staring intently at them. His hand clasped Sabrina's suddenly, and she knew that he wanted her to play along with him. They both stayed stock still, wordlessly becoming a part of the display. The little boy continued to gaze solemnly at the two Indians who had moved only moments before.

"Are you a real Indian?" he asked, but Colin and Sabrina remained perfectly still. "Hey," the boy nudged Colin. "Can'tcha talk?" He got no response, and after a few moments he ran back to his group, pointing back excitedly at the two immobile Indians. Colin and Sabrina watched him settle back into the class under the teacher's gentle guidance, and then their conversation continued.

"Desk job," he repeated. "Okay, call it what you want. It's a good base for me."

"It sounds like you're thinking about staying in one place."

He nodded. "You're right. But New York is the only place that won't bore me after a while, so here I am."

"But you still find time for an expedition or two?"

He glanced at the scar on his hand and smiled at her. "I'm looking forward to my next one with you." She smiled back, and he leaned over impulsively to give her a fleeting kiss. But he was forced to stop midway across the campfire as the little boy came racing back, dragging his teacher and pointing insistently.

"See? See?" he called. "Look! They're going to kiss!" The teached followed calmly, her face a mask of skeptical amusement, and the other kids giggled wildly at the boy's remark. The two Indians remained frozen partly out of instinct and partly out of embarrassment.

"They're not moving," a little girl in pigtails announced with authority. "They're just dummies, you dummy."

This was met by more giggles and a stern "Shhh!" from the teacher. " 'Lakota Campfire'," the teacher read from the plaque next to the display. "Hmmm, must be a wedding or something."

Sabrina's lips began to twitch, and she caught a little boy gazing at her solemnly. She couldn't resist giving him a fast wink.

"She moved!" the boy gasped.

"Aw, she did not," the others chorused.

"All right, children, let's line up and move on," the teacher announced with authority. The class fell noisily into a straggly line and she shepherded them out of the hall.

Colin and Sabrina burst out laughing, and he wrapped his arms around her and gave her a long, sweet kiss. "I just couldn't bear to break the spell," he sighed. "I wanted those kids to think we were real."

"I know," she answered, and then nudged him in the ribs. "But you don't believe in magic, right?"

His only response was to lean over to kiss her again, but he stopped when he caught sight of the teacher looking back curiously from the next gallery.

She looked perfectly aghast as he waved gaily, giving her a broad smile.

As he walked Sabrina outside, he reminded her that the following day would be the Mangia Society picnic—and the fossil hunt.

"I know," she answered coyly. "And tonight, if I work late, I'll finish my assignment at Lloyd's."

He stopped in the middle of the sidewalk and looked at her. "Tonight? Really?" She nodded. "In that case," he announced, "I think we should celebrate. Where would you like to dine this evening, madame?"

"Tavern on the Green," she answered without hesitation. "I want to dine in Central Park under the stars. Tomorrow is such an important day that I want to make a wish on my favorite star."

In front of the museum, Colin hailed a cab and Sabrina stepped inside, calling out, "Pick me up at ten o'clock!" He nodded as the cab sped off, and she went back to tackle the last of her week-long chore. By the time he arrived later that night, she was putting the finishing touches on the last of the windows.

"Incredible," he exclaimed, looking all around the main floor. What had been the cosmetics department had been transformed by the crew into a sophisticated survey of face paint from other cultures. A large model of the Plains Indian chief stood next to one counter, splendidly bedecked in war paint and eagle feathers. The Indian looked magnificent and proud, somehow not at all out of place. Oversized palettes of colors were placed at various points next to mirrors, so that customers could try different color combinations, and the odd shapes lent a festive, art decor air to the displays. "Incredible," Colin repeated as he wandered through a maze of prisms that caught a sparkling array of colors from every angle.

Sabrina led him inside the windows, where once

again he was rendered speechless. Neanderthal men and women dressed in skins stood next to sleek mannequins in fur coats, walking dinosaurs on long leashes. There were papier maché caves and real campfires waiting to be lit, and painted backdrops suggesting the Paleozoic era. Colin didn't realize it, but a charmed smile lingered on his face as he examined her handiwork. "Completely anachronistic," he said to himself, "but for some reason, the whole thing works." He kept shaking his head and looking around in disbelief, finally sitting down on a fake tree stump that faced Fifth Avenue.

"Surprised?" she asked quietly, sitting down next to him on a rock.

"You've done a marvelous job, Sabrina," he said sincerely. "I must say, I didn't think it would work." He looked up into the open mouth of the tyrannosaurus rex model. "I thought it would be . . . well . . ."

"Tasteless?" she supplied helpfully, suppressing a smile.

He stood up, ducking to avoid the tyrannosaurus's head. "You can decorate my cave any time."

They went back into the store and he reached for a large bouquet of flowers that he had left on a counter. "I almost forgot," he said, bowing gallantly. "These are for you. A lady in flight."

"Oh, Colin. They're beautiful!" She buried her nose in the blossoms and took a deep breath. "Mmmm . . . heavenly." Looking up with a radiant face, she added, "And I'm finished here! Finished!" She spun around lightly on one foot. "Forever!" she shouted into the empty store.

Colin was watching her, amused and happy. "Now you're a full-fledged professional artist," he reminded her. "And a famous one at that."

"I am, aren't I?" she said softly. Then, as the reality sank in, she repeated, "I am!"

Her excitement was contagious. Colin took her firmly by the hand and announced, "We're going out to celebrate. Come on!"

They got as far as the exit when he peered outside and stopped. "Uh—there's just one minor problem."

"What is it?" she asked anxiously.

"Well . . . I've got good news and I've got bad news for you." He scratched his chin. "The good news is that we're dining under the stars, all right."

Sabrina frowned. "And the bad news?" she asked suspiciously.

He didn't answer, but pushed the door open and gestured up at the sky. "Not one star," he said flatly.

The air was chilly. "Mm," she confirmed, trying to stifle her disappointment. "Look at those clouds."

Colin smiled mischievously, and she pounced on him, knowing that he was hiding something. "Why do I have the feeling that you've got something up your sleeve?" she demanded.

His grin became devilish. "I promised you we'd dine under the stars tonight. And we will." He stole a glance at her to see if she understood, but she regarded him with the same look of distrust. "But first we'll have to stop off and pick up a little something for a nocturnal picnic."

She questioned him to no avail, and ten minutes later they were heading uptown in his truck, bouncing over the potholes. But when he pulled up in front of a two-story delicatessen and gourmet shop, she turned to him with reluctant protest. It was obviously crowded, even at this late hour, and the astonishing collection of fresh and imported food and equipment practically spilled out onto the sidewalk. You could smell the food before you actually got inside; a thousand different tantalizing aromas wafted out to the street.

"Is this your idea of a place to stop for 'a little something?' " she asked. "I know better than to come here when I'm hungry. I'll end up buying out the entire store."

They walked inside and were immediately assaulted by the full effect of the aroma. Various counters spaced throughout the densely crowded store featured imported chocolates, pastries still warm from the oven, a huge array of wedges and rounds of cheeses, rows of meats and smoked fish, fat salamis hung on cords from the ceiling, freshly cut pasta, an entire wall of coffee and tea blends, unusual appetizers fresh from the busy kitchen, and imports from every country on earth. Sabrina stalked through it all like a general with a battle plan, her green eyes gleaming as she planned an impromptu but lush menu.

The first stop was the fish counter, where she chose a few razor-sharp slices of succulent smoked salmon. Then they sampled several cheeses, finally settling on a brisk Gouda and a creamy white cheese laced with crushed pistachios. The rich display of appetizers presented a problem, but finally they settled on a piquant broccoli and zucchini salad, a small mushroom quiche, and curried ground lamb wrapped in phyllo dough. After carefully perusing the elegant varieties of chocolate, they chose Belgian truffles wrapped in gold foil and two fluted raspberry creams.

Standing in line at the cashier, they looked like two thieves carrying stolen diamonds. The purchases were heaped into a large shopping bag, and after a quick stop at a nearby liquor store for a cold bottle of champagne, they piled back into the truck, laughing like two kids playing hookey from school.

"I told you I wouldn't be able to stop," she said gleefully. "I can't wait to eat all this up. Just where is this heavenly place you promised?"

He smiled mysteriously. "We're almost there," he said as he drove around the corner.

Four blocks later he pulled into the parking lot of the Museum of Natural History, and Sabrina groaned elaborately in disappointment. "Oh, Colin!" she protested, twisting around in her seat to face him. "Is this your idea of a romantic setting? Don't you ever think about anyplace else?"

"Stop complaining," he said cheerfully. "Follow me." He helped her down from the truck and they went inside, confronting the now-familiar specters of black bears and horned moose, motionless but still ferocious in their glass cases. Sabrina expected to be taken up to his office, but instead he led her down another hallway on the first floor. In a moment he produced a set of keys and unlocked a door. "After you," he said, gesturing in the shadows.

Sabrina stepped in hesitantly and met with complete and total blackness. "Where are we?" she whispered.

"Shhh," he warned, closing the door behind them. "No one knows I have this key. We're not really supposed to be in here."

"In *where*?" The absolute darkness was unnerving, and she was beginning to feel frightened.

"Give me your hand." He groped around, finding her hand and imprisoning her fingers in his own. Sabrina turned back involuntarily, but all she could see was the red exit sign over the door. He tugged on her hand and they inched forward, their feet encounting carpeting after a few steps. Colin bumped into something hard. "Ow!" he cried, stopping abruptly.

"Talk about the blind leading the blind," Sabrina mumbled.

"Quiet, Elf," he said, pulling her forward. "We're almost there." He turned suddenly, finding an open space. "Step down," he commanded, and she did, realizing that they were going down a set of stairs. Her hand flailed out and touched something velvety that felt like a chair. She groped around. It *was* a chair. A step later, she felt another chair.

"Are we in a theater of some kind?" she asked, breaking the utter stillness.

"Wait there." He let go of her hand and disappeared into the depths of the blackness.

"Colin!" she called out. He didn't answer. "Colin?"

She could hear him negotiating the last few steps, and then his shoes were on linoleum again, his footsteps ringing in the silence. He stopped and began to grope around, his hands banging into things that neither one of them could see. "Where is that switch . . ." he muttered. "I know it's here somewhere." He continued to search while Sabrina stood gripping the side of a chair. "Ah!" he exclaimed suddenly. "Here it is!"

And as he spoke, the circular room became ethereally visible, lit from above with the lights of hundreds upon hundreds of tiny stars.

"The planetarium!" Sabrina gasped, her head bent back as she gazed upward. It was as if the roof of the museum had been suddenly removed, revealing a full summer night's sky in all of its radiant splendor. Sabrina looked all around the glittering dome, her eyes traveling slowly in hushed awe.

"It's beautiful," she breathed.

As she stared, the entire dome began to move very slowly, the pageant of stars parading majestically across the blackness. Sabrina realized that she was leaning backwards as she watched it, and she was so mesmerized that she almost fell.

"Easy, there." Colin's strong arm swept behind her suddenly, and she straightened up, glad for the support. He led her down to the center of the planetarium, and she made out a control panel covered with buttons and switches and tiny lights. He flicked a switch, and immediately the stars stopped moving.

"Delivered as promised," he said, reaching into the deli bag. "A picnic under the stars."

Sabrina remained speechless as he took out all of the food and placed it on the control panel. Plastic forks and knives came last, along with paper plates and napkins, but the crowning glory was the bottle of champagne, still pleasantly cold. She watched him as he struggled with the top, pulling it up, and then there was the loud popping sound as it sailed into the air. He poured two glasses and handed her one.

"To Sabrina Melendey," he said grandly, his voice bouncing off the opposite wall. "Artist *extra-ordinaire*."

They clinked glasses wordlessly, the sound echoing softly in the dark, empty room. The chilled champagne was delightfully smooth as it coursed gently through Sabrina's body. Its sparkle seemed to illuminate her, making her green eyes glow with anticipation. The whole setting was magical, and she felt that somehow, something wonderful was about to happen.

"Let's start with the salmon," he said, breaking into her reverie. The smoky taste of the fish enhanced the illusion that they were outside, as if they were seated around a campfire instead of a control panel. Colin pressed a button, and a full moon rose to reign over the night sky.

"Did you want to wish on a star?" he asked with a smile as they started on the salad and the quiche.

"What?" she asked absently, biting into a tangy bit of broccoli coated with garlic dressing. "Oh! Oh, yes," she added seriously, her eyes scanning the profusion of stars above them.

"Which one do you want to wish on?" He picked up a flashlight with a pointer and aimed it up at the dome. A small but distinct green arrow appeared against the blackness, waiting for a direction. "Pick a star, any star."

"Which is the brightest?" she asked in a whisper.

"Sirius." The green arrow flew across the dome and stopped next to a large and beautiful star. "Go on, make a wish," he said. Sabrina said nothing, but her eyes glowed. Silently she wished that she would always feel as peaceful and full of wonder as she did at that moment. She shut her eyes for a moment, relishing the brief intensity.

"What did you wish?" Colin asked after a pause.

"I can't tell you," she teased, reaching for a piece of phyllo. She took a large bite, savoring the warm, spicy flavor blending with the flaky crust. "If I tell, it won't come true."

Colin smiled and poured more champagne. He pressed another button on the control board, and as if by magic, a gigantic ball of shimmery light appeared, dwarfing even the full moon.

"What's that?" she asked, stunned.

"That's a nova," he explained. "A star that has gone wild, exploding within itself."

She stared. "But why?"

"Because it's dying. This is its last magnificent show of light." He smiled poignantly. "Stars know how to go out in style."

They watched in silence for a while, nibbling on the quiche and sipping champagne.

"Show me a constellation," she said at last.

Obligingly, the green arrow darted across the dome, and stopped at a small cluster of stars. "Aquarius," he announced. "The water bearer."

"Aquarius!" she cried. "That's my zodiac sign!" She turned to him, impressed. "How did you know that?"

"I didn't," he shrugged. "I took a wild guess. I don't believe in astrology, Sabrina."

She sighed. "Oh, Colin. Don't you ever let go? Don't you ever have flights of fancy?"

He came up behind her and put his hands on her

arms. "In my own way. But not with magic and hocus-pocus."

She sighed again and decided to let it pass. "Show me another constellation."

The arrow whizzed along, halting beside another group of stars. "Sculptoris," he said.

"Sculptoris?" she frowned. "What's that?"

"The sculptor!" he replied.

Sabrina didn't believe him. "You made that up," she insisted. "There is no such constellation."

"Yes there is," he returned calmly. "Would you like me to show you a chart?"

"Later," she hedged.

"Well, how about this?" In a twinkling, the radiant tail of a comet went gliding gracefully across the night sky, brightening the planetarium and casting a luminous glow across their faces.

"It's so beautiful," she said reverently. "I could never paint anything as magnificent as that."

"No one could," he said simply. "That's the whole point. Don't you see?"

"See what?"

He swallowed the last piece of quiche and pressed her arms. "I don't need flights of fancy, Sabrina. Not when I have this. To me, the miracles of nature are wondrous enough. You see that star over there?" He pointed. "They think that a planet resembling earth might be in orbit around it. A planet that's millions of years behind us in evolution, but with the potential for life as we know it. Think of it! We're spinning around a star in the middle of infinity, and yet we are able to reach out into the vastness and look for answers to questions that have remained unanswered for centuries." His hands gripped her arms in excitement. "But there will always be more questions, and our descendants, whoever they are and whatever they look like, will still be trying to answer them." He sighed almost breathlessly. "That's why I don't look for magic, Sabrina. Because I find it every day right in front of my eyes."

She turned in his arms and faced him, her eyes shining. "I never thought of it that way." Leaning forward on her toes, she planted a light but warm kiss on his mouth. He returned the kiss with one of his own, and they stopped and looked at each other solemnly for a long moment. Then he kissed her again, but this time it was long and deep and full of intensity. His tongue sought the inside of her mouth as his hands pressed her slender back. She was forced to lean back as he bent over her, her breasts straining up to crush against his chest as her body arched. His sudden ardor didn't surprise her, because she was experiencing the same reaction to the unexpected connection they had just made.

Even though the desire rising through her was familiar, Sabrina was electrified by a new and tremulous awareness. Maybe, just maybe, this man had more to offer her than she had thought. Maybe there was more than the lightning green eyes that always seemed to look through her, the lean, irresistible body, and the quick, agile mind so dedicated to his work. She had discovered that he was an adventurer, but the full scope of his exploration had escaped her. He found excitement not only in the remote corners of the earth—he found it everywhere he looked.

But any further thought was lost as he showered light, arousing kisses over her cheeks, her nose, her ears, and her throat, leaving a fiery path of response. She clung to him, feeling the rapid beat of her heart through the thin fabric of her dress. His hands became hungry and demanding, roaming over her body in a way that told her just how fiercely he wanted her. Her breasts flamed instantly, as she knew they would. The delicate peaks grew taut under his circling fingertips, sending shafts of desire shooting down her body. And his knowing hands followed the shafts, tracing sensuous lines around the womanly curve of her waist and reaching behind to tease the fullness in back.

He bunched the material of her dress and lifted it so that he could find the softness underneath. Her thighs were warm and yielding. Colin placed one finger between them, moving it upward very slowly. He ceased all other strokes, letting this one provocative gesture command the way to the center of her desire. Sabrina's head fell back as she waited and waited for him to reach it, but he did not. She could feel her nipples straining against her dress, could sense the sweet honey that was being rendered from her very core. His finger, still deep between her thighs, traveled up and up, until her knees became weak and her legs began to tremble. She tried to lean against him, and he drew her down onto the carpeted floor of the planetarium, supporting her back with one arm.

At last the teasing finger found its mark, sliding easily inside her body and out again before concentrating on tiny strokes that ignited her beyond all reason. Sabrina cried out, helpless under the liquid rush of sensation. She wanted it to last and last even as she wanted the exquisite torment to end. Her eyes opened fleetingly and caught the profusion of sparkling stars shining overhead, and it seemed to make perfect sense that they were there. Her eyes closed again as she drank in the silky fire of his touch.

She wanted to sit up, to unbutton his shirt, to shower him with the same kind of pleasure he was giving her. But when he drew the thin straps of her dress down her sloping shoulders and gently kissed the pouting roundness of one breast, she was unable to do anything except surrender. His mouth played delicately with the pale pink nipple, and this, combined with the highly charged strokes of his hand, sent her toppling over the edge, her hips arching unconsciously as the world spun madly around her.

He waited quietly until her breathing slowed. When at last her eyes fluttered open to gaze upward at the glittering dome, he caught both her hands in his and looked down at her. "You elf," he said, his eyes flashing. "Don't you know that there is nothing more real than this?"

She sighed luxuriously, her body still trembling, and he moved over her suddenly, as graceful as a panther. His mouth came down on hers, tasting her sweetness. When it lifted, his face was lined with an intensity she had never seen there before. Sabrina held him tightly, straining her body against him. They began to rock slightly with the motion, so that he flipped over and she immediately straddled him, determined to have her way.

The buttons of his shirt opened quickly under her touch, leaving his bronzed chest bare. She raked the smooth skin with her nails, making him shiver slightly, and she bent her head to tease the male nipples with her tongue. They responded as quickly as her own did, tightening as she tugged them gently with her teeth. The rest of his clothes followed, as she slowly drew his pants down his long, hard legs. Her hands were like two butterflies, roaming deftly over his body, and her mouth stopped to add intensity where her hands had only teased. He groaned and writhed sensuously under her spell, and she relished the power she had over him at that moment.

"God, woman, you're like magic," he uttered breathlessly.

Sabrina couldn't resist a tiny smile. "I thought you didn't believe in magic, Colin. Only reality . . ."

His eyes flew open, shooting dangerous sparks. Her teasing laugh was cut short as he sat up and pushed her back, pinning her hips to the floor. "Nothing can ever be more real than this," he said hoarsely. "We're never more alive, more real, more vital in this universe than when we are making love."

His last few words were muffled as he lowered his head to tease the small roundness of her belly with little circles of his tongue. He tasted the light sheen on her body as he worked his way upward, kissing the space between her breasts and the hollow of her throat.

Sabrina was on fire again, her hips moving in broken circles on the floor. Her legs opened to receive him, but he was in charge now, accepting her blatant invitation. He positioned himself above her, his muscular arms pressing against the carpet, his long legs stretched out between her open ones, his narrow hips finding the exact location that would unite her body with his.

When he was ready, he lodged his hardness against her, but paused, delaying the fundamental heart of their union until her eyes flew open, pleading and demanding him to complete their bond.

"Nothing can ever be more real than this," he repeated. And with those words he pressed forward, entering her with calculated deliberation that filled her and expanded her in a way she had never thought possible. The inside of her body sang, flooding her with release. She felt completely lush, like a garden in full bloom.

And the torment only spiraled as she received the force of his rhythmic thrusts. Her legs wrapped themselves around his back in passionate effort to hold him even closer. Faster and faster they moved, with never a break in rhythm, until at last they were shaken by the shattering explosion that spun crazily out of control.

"I feel like we've just been to the moon and back," she said jokingly as she opened her eyes and saw the full moon. "Are you sure we're not floating in some kind of spaceship?"

Colin smiled and left a warm, lingering kiss on her

mouth. "I'm afraid jet propulsion doesn't quite work that way. But this is just as good."

Sabrina reflected on that answer as the truck drove higher and higher into the mountains, and she stole a sidelong glance at Colin's sharply defined face. Jet propulsion! What a thing to say at such a moment! But that was Colin. She smiled a little as she realized she was getting used to his odd remarks, almost fond of them. And she stifled a tiny sigh as she thought of how effortlessly he could arouse her, and of how alive he looked when he was talking about one of his expeditions. He was the most intelligent man she had ever known, but his intelligence always seemed to be focused on something beyond her reach.

He caught her staring at him, and smiled. She was so beautiful. So mercurial. And so hopelessly romantic. It was as if she were living in some kind of artist's never-never land, refusing to completely grow up. Except that when he made love to her, she was all woman. Never had he known such passion and vibrancy.

"Penny for your thoughts," she said quietly.

"I was thinking about you," he answered boldly. He paused. "A nickel for yours."

"Mine?" She was startled, suddenly bashful. Should she tell him that she had just been reliving last night's scene in the planetarium? A warm little tingle passed through her body as she remembered how very deeply she had responded. It seemed that every cell had been awakened and stimulated by his touch.

"I was thinking about you, too," she said at last, giving him a mysterious little smile.

That was safe enough. But the problem was, she didn't know if she'd ever be able to stop thinking about him at all.

Chapter Eight

The road became steeper and steeper as they drove higher, and Colin downshifted the truck. Sabrina was clutching a map of the area, but with the sharp turns and frequent bumps she also had to hold on to the bar of the door. All around them, the lush green forest covered the mountainside. The pines and firs and evergreens grew densely, towering proudly over the road. Occasionally a small clearing would afford them a brief, tantalizing glimpse of the valley below, but the winding road often played tricks on their eyes, letting them see only sun-dappled spaces in the forest.

"So tell me," Colin said conversationally. "How many people are expected at this picnic?"

"I don't know," she answered vaguely, watching as a mountain peak came into view at the top of the road. They were almost at the summit, and thin wisps of clouds floated lazily in the air.

He frowned. "Well, what I mean is, will there be enough people to be able to conduct a methodical search of the area? I was up last night after you fell asleep, and I drew some graphs." His right hand rummaged on the seat next to him. He found a bunch of papers, pulled one out and handed it to her. "Here," he said.

She looked down at it and then looked up at him curiously. His gaze was focused on the road, so she looked back at the map he had drawn, rather awed at its exactness. It was a simple, homemade map, but he had used precision tools, and the result was a neat rendering that looked almost printed. "This looks like something out of my high school geometry class," she remarked.

He remained unperturbed. "We'll start here," he said, pointing to a spot on the map. She saw that he had sectioned off various areas, and he had pointed to the section marked "A."

"This is what kept you up half the night?" she asked curiously.

"Of course. We've got to go about this scientifically, or there isn't any point in doing it. Can't waste time, can we?" He threw her a brisk grin. "Besides, if we don't cover the whole area today, I'll know where to start when I come back tomorrow."

"Tomorrow?" Now she was really surprised. She had only seen signs of his dedication before. Now she was seeing it in action. "How long do you intend to search for this thing?"

It was his turn to be surprised. "Until I find it." His answer sounded very definite, and she sat back in her seat and suppressed a frown.

"You know," she began carefully. "Tomorrow morning is the reception at Lloyd's to celebrate the opening of the new displays. You're invited as the representative from the museum."

"Hey!" he said suddenly, startling her. "Didn't you say that your friend Veronica is an oceanographer?"

She nodded, puzzled.

"I wonder if she knows anything about ancient lakes in this region," he mumbled, half to himself.

"Colin!"

"What?"

"You weren't even listening to me."

"What? Oh! Sure I was. You were saying that tomorrow morning is the reception at Lloyd's. I know, I received an invitation." He gave her another one of those brisk smiles. "Why don't we worry about that later? We may find something here today, and then it won't even be a problem." The truck negotiated a very sharp curve, and they both leaned perilously to the right. "Just breathe that mountain air!" he exclaimed heartily. "It's almost as clear as the air in the Himalayas, but not quite. After all, the Himalayas don't suffer from our pollution."

"When were you in the Himalayas?" she asked.

"Oh, a few years ago. I want you to show me exactly where you got that hunk of limestone. It's very important. I'll need samples of that rock."

Sabrina did not bother to disguise her impatience. "You really have a one-track mind today, don't you?"

Colin nodded emphatically. "Yes."

She gave up then and concentrated on the ride, which was becoming slower and more scenic. There were more breaks in the trees, allowing spectacular views through the clearings, and the wind blew steadily across the road. Even the air seemed cooler at this altitude. Sabrina guessed that it was easily ten degrees cooler here than in the city.

"Tell me," he said suddenly, picking up on his current thought. "Did you tell anyone to bring hammers and magnifying glasses?"

"No," she sighed. "I didn't tell them to bring anything except food."

He nodded thoughtfully. "Well, that's all right. I have about twenty hammers in the truck and maybe a hundred hand magnifiers." He squinted, considering. "But I'm sure some of them will have thought to bring hammers, at least."

"I doubt that," she said dryly. "None of them will have much use for a hammer at a French country picnic."

He was unmovable, like a reporter tracking down a

lead. "But they know the purpose of this gathering, right? You did tell them?"

She shifted uncomfortably, sensing that he wouldn't like her answer. She was right; he guessed it immediately.

"Do you mean to tell me that all those people are coming all the way up here for a picnic? Nothing more?"

"What's wrong with that?" She turned to face him, her face drawn back in irritation.

"What's wrong with that?" he repeated incredulously. "What's wrong with it is that it's crazy. And what's more, you practically lied to them. They're all being duped into doing something they know nothing about!"

"That doesn't matter," she tried to explain. "The purpose of the Mangia Society is to enjoy great food and to have a good time. And if you ask them to join in a fossil hunt, I'm sure they'll be more than happy—"

"You mean this is all some kind of game to you?" He swerved to avoid a rabbit that hopped across the road, and they both clung to the seat.

"A game!"

"Well, what else would you call it?" The truck swerved back onto course, jolting them up out of their seats for a moment.

"Are you quite finished?" she asked icily.

"No." His voice was stony, and she felt uneasy through her anger. She had never seen him like this before. "You know what your problem is, Sabrina?"

"No. What?"

"You have absolutely no sense of organization. Everything is just a lark to you. You don't care about deadlines, and you think that anything not related to your great pursuit of art is irrelevant. No wonder you were so late in getting to the Lloyd's exhibit. You left it until the very last minute."

She let him have his say, but she was steaming. "Stop the truck," she ordered him tersely.

"Don't be silly. We're miles from—"

"I know where we are. Stop the truck. Now!"

He jammed the brakes angrily, throwing both of them forward. She gave him a defiant glare and jumped out, slamming the door behind her. Colin remained sitting in the truck, and she began to walk up the incline, her feet crunching the ground in the silence.

What gave him the right to make judgments about her? Of all the nerve! Here they were, about to enjoy a magnificent day, and he could think only about his own pursuits. He accused her of being interested only in art? Hah! He should take a look in the mirror sometime if he wanted a good picture of narrow-mindedness. Her thoughts tumbled furiously, one upon the other, when suddenly she heard the rumble of the truck behind her. He drove up slowly beside her and kept the vehicle at her pace as she strode along.

"May I say one more thing?" he asked levelly.

"Haven't you said enough?" She quickened her pace, but of course he only sped up, catching up with her a few feet ahead. She decided to ignore him completely, but he stepped on the accelerator suddenly, pulling ahead and then stopping about thirty feet up the road. To her dismay, he turned off the engine and leaped out. He stood leaning casually against the side of the truck, waiting for her to meet him.

She couldn't turn back, and she couldn't just stand there. There was no choice but to march past him.

"Sabrina," he said calmly when she approached. She tried her best to stare straight ahead, but she felt suddenly ridiculous, and she stopped and faced him. "Isn't it possible that we're both wrong?" he asked mildly. His eyes watched her intently, and she felt her façade beginning to crumble.

"It's possible," she said, struggling to maintain it. "But highly doubtful."

He laughed loudly, his clear voice echoing through the trees. "You mean I'm right?"

She opened her mouth in protest, and he interrupted whatever she was about to say. "A joke, Sabrina. Albeit a feeble one. Don't tell me you have no sense of humor."

"What? Me? No sense of humor?" She bristled, almost speechless. "Are you serious? That's one thing I have plenty of, Mr. Scientist. In fact, I happen to be an expert in that area."

The amusement danced across his strong features, and she stopped short. She realized that he was teasing her, and she was falling for the bait. Confused, she fell silent, not knowing what to say next.

"May I ask you one simple question?" he queried.

She frowned. "What?"

"Why didn't you tell anyone that a fossil hunt was going to be a big part of the day's activities?"

It was a simple enough question, but she had to think about it. The answer rose quickly, but she looked down, reluctant to tell him.

"Well?" he prodded gently.

She looked up and faced him, her mouth set in a small line of determination. "Because I didn't think anyone would want to come if they knew about it," she answered truthfully. "The Mangia Society is supposed to create *joie de vivre*. It's not supposed to be an eighth grade field trip."

There it was again. Colin winced slightly, staring at her coldly. She had absolutely no interest in his work, and she saw nothing wrong with saying so.

"Are you saying that this search would be too tedious?" he asked, trying to be fair.

"No, I'm saying that it would be too boring."

His eyes filled with anger, and she drew back,

alarmed. "Did I say something wrong?" she wondered aloud.

"You can drop that innocent expression! It doesn't become you, Sabrina."

"What are you talking about?" She was genuinely puzzled, and he shook his head pessimistically.

"I am talking about the fact that you are completely insensitive to my work, that's what. For all your artistic sensibilities, you're not too perceptive when it comes to someone else's feelings." Her face changed rapidly as she absorbed his words. "That's right, Sabrina," he went on, noting her discomfort. "You, the sensitive artist."

"Colin," she said, subdued. "You're not being reasonable. Don't you see? I couldn't dump the idea of a fossil hunt on everyone just like that. They wouldn't have gone for it."

He regarded her coolly. "And what makes you think they'll go for it up here?"

"Oh," she waved a hand airily, dismissing the whole thing. "They'll go for it. Don't worry. If we announce it in just the right way, they'll think the whole thing is fun."

"Fun," he repeated glumly. "Fun, fun, fun. Somehow, this whole group sounds hopelessly hedonistic to me."

"It is," she agreed, smiling coyly. "That's the whole idea. Don't you believe in simple pleasures?" Her look was deliberately suggestive, and he couldn't help smiling back.

"Sometimes," he hedged, but they were both smiling now, and they knew that the argument was over. Not resolved, but at least it was over for now. A gentle but persistent breeze wafted over them, smoothing away the ruffled edges. Sabrina couldn't stay angry with him, and he melted, knowing as he looked down at her endlessly fascinating face that he couldn't hope to win an argument with her. Not here, in this unearthly setting. Their differences would simply have to wait.

Thirty minutes later, after meeting at the rendez-vous point in the nearest town, they were standing in the middle of the flower-filled meadow, the breeze ruffling their hair. The air was fragrant with the perfume of the flowers and the surrounding pines. Sabrina took a long, deep breath and sighed extravagantly.

"Ah!" she exclaimed. "Isn't it wonderful?"

Cars were pulling up behind them, and people were walking into the meadow to join them. Colin looked around curiously. "There must have been fifty cars back there," he mused. "Don't tell me that all those people are coming up here for a picnic!"

"Of course they are!" a voice said gaily. They turned and saw Allegra standing there holding a silver tray. "Have a canapé," she offered graciously. Her enthusiasm and joy were contagious. Colin smiled affably and took a canapé, biting into it politely. Then his face lit up in surprise.

"Hey!" he said, turning to her. "This is good! What is it?"

Allegra laughed and winked. "Professional secret," she said. "But recipes are available to members of the Mangia Society. Would you like to join?"

He looked surprised, but he nodded gamely. "Sure. I'm here as Sabrina's guest. What do I have to do, fill out an application?"

"I'll send you all the particulars when we get back to New York. Sabrina will give me your address . . . won't you, Sabrina?" She trilled another laugh and mingled her way through the growing crowd.

"Was she just teasing, or what?" Colin asked.

"She—uh—thinks I'm kind of sweet on you," Sabrina answered rather lamely.

"Oh."

The awkward pause that followed was broken

when Colin caught sight of Veronica coming toward them. She was dressed in khaki trousers, a plaid shirt, a denim jacket, and sturdy boots. A small magnifying glass hung on a cord around her neck. She held a hammer in one hand and a canapé in the other.

"Hi," she said jovially, waving the hammer in greeting. "So where's the mysterious missing link? I'm all set for the big hunt."

Colin looked at Sabrina in delighted surprise, but she only gave him a blank look. "I didn't tell her anything," she said, baffled. "Allegra must have mentioned something to her."

Colin warmed immediately to the one person who was obviously on his wavelength. "I hope we'll find another rogericus here today," he said to Veronica. "If we do, it will provide the answers to a lot of questions about the evolution of amphibians into reptiles."

Veronica nodded. "Are you familiar with the foot sample in Ontario?"

"Yes, yes I am," he beamed. "We're looking for the whole animal today."

"Really?" Her eyes widened.

He nodded eagerly. "I have some sketches in my truck, if you'd like to see them."

"I certainly would." They walked off together, talking a mile a minute. Sabrina was left standing there, looking after them with very mixed feelings. She heard Colin say something about organic compounds, and she frowned.

"Organic compounds," Sabrina muttered darkly. "Lovely."

"You really like that guy, don't you?" It was Allegra, and she was smiling knowingly.

"Oh, I don't know," she answered evasively.

"Well, I do," Allegra smiled. "Come on. The food is all set up. I hope you're hungry."

Sabrina cast one more glance back at Colin, who was showing Veronica one of his graphs. But the lure of one of Allegra's famous spreads proved too tempting to resist, and Sabrina walked across the meadow to where long tables had been set up.

The tables were at the edge of the mountain summit, overlooking the entire valley. The first few picnickers were already loading their plates with food, but Sabrina took a moment to marvel at the incredible view. She could see whole towns nestled in the foothills, the steeples of churches poking up like beacons. Small lakes shone like jewels, reflecting the light of the sun, and rivers snaked through the panorama, rushing into each other and down to the sea. The scene looked like a reproduction of a picture postcard, but no postcard could have captured the radiant play of light and shadow, nor the exquisite checkerboard patterns of the farmland and the forest.

Sabrina's artist's mind automatically started blending colors and eyeing contours, planning how she would paint such a scene. It was difficult to know where to look first, and she shook her head in awe.

"Magnificent," she said aloud. "Truly magnificent."

"Magnificent, isn't it?" came Colin's voice from behind. He stepped up and joined her, standing next to her on the cliff.

"I was just thinking how I would paint this view," she said softly.

"Mmmm," he nodded thoughtfully. "But what would you paint? What do you see?" His eyes were dreamy as he stared into the valley.

She took a deep breath. "I see colors and patterns and shapes. I see purple shadows, not black. I see an endless diffusion of sunlight." She paused. "I'd paint the essence as I see it. Like *Lady in Flight*—the essence of movement. The essence here is—"

"Movement," he broke in.

"No, no," she said impatiently. "That was *Lady in Flight*. This is a landscape. It's stationary."

He laughed quietly. "Nothing could be further from the truth." Walking forward to the very edge of the summit, he pointed. "You see all those cliffs? They weren't always here, and one day they'll be gone forever."

"What are you talking about?"

His eyes roamed avidly over the area. "The earth is in constant motion, Sabrina. It looks stationary because we spend such a short time on it. But this planet is still very young." He turned to her, growing more excited. "Do you know how these mountains were formed? They were pushed upward by the massive, churning force of the earth in its infancy. And when the upheaval was over, the glaciers came through, carving massive paths thousands of miles wide."

She stared, wide-eyed. "And when did all this stop?"

"That's just the point. It didn't. It never stops. These mountains are beautiful, aren't they? Well, take a good look at them, because they won't always be here. Some other force or phenomenon will come along to change the map again. Look down."

"What?"

"Look down," he commanded. "Right where we're standing. This used to be a riverbed."

She stared down as if expecting to see water washing up around her ankles.

He hunkered down and ran his hand across the ground, scooping up a handful of stones. "Aha!" he exclaimed, standing up again. "You see?"

"See what?" She peered at the stones. They looked like ordinary stones.

"Look closely," he said, picking one out and pointing at a series of tiny lines embedded in it. "This is the footprint of an ancient clam."

She grabbed it and examined it, running a nail along the tiny, perfect ridges. "My God," she breathed. "How old is this thing?"

He shrugged and threw it down. "Oh, ten million years. Not very old at all, considering."

"What are you doing?" she cried, falling to the ground to retrieve the fossil. "Don't throw it away. I want to keep it!"

Colin looked at her, pleased beyond measure. "I'm glad you like it," he said simply.

"So this is an ancient clam," she said reverently, shaking her head in wonder.

"No," he explained patiently. "This isn't the clam. The clam disintegrated long ago. This is the impression it left. It's an exact copy, though." He smiled. "You don't mind a copy, do you?"

"Not at all. This is every bit as good." Her eyes were shining as she looked at her find. Her hands cupped it lovingly, and she put it carefully in her pocket.

"Unfortunately," he remarked, "that piece is only ten million years old—much younger than what I'm looking for. Later on I'll hand out sketches of large shells that are three hundred and fifty million years old—the same age as our missing link. It will be easiest to look for those, because of their size and because they're likely to be plentiful. And when we find some, we'll know we've hit the right spot. Then we'll be able to concentrate on that area."

She nodded and asked, "But don't you want me to show you the exact location of the limestone I used to make *Lady in Flight*?"

"That's the first place we'll look before wasting any time," he agreed. "But I'm afraid it's not something to count on. I have a funny feeling about that stone, but we'll give it a try." He turned back to face the meadow. "Come on, Elf. I'm hungry."

They walked to the other end of the ledge, where a
group had gathered around the long tables that
Allegra had set up. She stood behind the display of
food wearing a shopkeeper's smile. A large white
chef's hat was perched on her dark curls, and her
small frame was covered by a voluminous white
apron. She pointed at the various dishes as they
looked on in admiration. Behind her, the spectacular
panorama of the valley and the mountains beyond
framed the lush scene. Snowcapped peaks were visible in the distance, some lost in the clouds.

Allegra had chosen to decorate the lavish spread
with the wild flowers that were growing profusely in
the meadow. Fresh, dewy cornflowers, daisies, but-
tercups, and Queen Anne's lace were arranged in
blue china vases, creating the impression that the
feast was homey and informal as well as elegant.

"We begin with the vichyssoise," she announced.
"That's a cold potato and leek soup, and it's very
smooth and creamy. Next comes a spicy sausage
wrapped in dough; I can cut you a large or a small
piece, depending on your appetite. The fish contri-
bution is pike dumplings with horseradish sauce.
And this," she continued, gesturing with a flourish,
"is my *pièce de résistance*—cold roast of veal stuffed
with wild rice. To go with it I have dilled carrots and
crusty French bread with sweet butter." She moved
down the line, Sabrina and Colin following on the
grass as they surveyed the abundance of food. "Fresh
grapes and figs are the light dessert, and I also have
pots de crème au chocolat with candied violets, in
case you don't mind the extra calories." She smiled
impishly, as if the elimination of the one rich dessert
could possibly make up for the ample bounty of her
table. "A bottle of light, dry white wine goes with it
all, and I have espresso and iced tea as well." Her
guests stood back, impressed. "Now," she said,
getting down to business. "What can I get you?"

They pointed, deliberated, and chose, letting her heap their plates with food.

"This looks absolutely delicious," Colin said as he looked down at his plate. "I can't believe I'm going to eat it all."

"You will," Allegra assured him, tucking her windblown curls underneath her chef's hat. "You may even be back for seconds."

"I know *I* always am," said a familiar voice.

They turned and saw Zeebo contemplating the array of food, his eyes gleaming with culinary anticipation. He was dressed in designer overalls with a red and white striped jersey shirt. Sabrina smiled and saluted her friend with a glass of wine. "When did you get here?" she asked.

"Just now," he replied in his level, Eastern-accented voice. "And just in time for the repast, it seems." He turned to Colin. "Ah, Mr. Forrester. How are you?" The two men shook hands. "Uh—I believe there's someone here who wants to talk to you." He jerked his head in the other direction, where Arthur Wellington was walking up the incline. "We drove up together. There's something Mr. Wellington wants to discuss with you."

"And I have a pretty good idea what it's about," Sabrina added nervously. "Don't get into a scene with him, Colin, all right?"

Colin turned to her with a look of mock innocence. "Me? Make a scene?" She was not amused, and he decided to humor her. "All right, all right, don't worry. I'll go and talk to him myself and get it over with if you like."

She considered. "Maybe that's a good idea."

He winked at her jauntily. "Be right back." Carrying his plate and a glass of chilled wine, he strode across the meadow to Arthur Wellington, who was just arriving at the picnic site.

"I believe I'll join them," Zeebo said. "This may be

too good to miss." Before she could stop him, he made his way across the grass.

Sabrina picked up one the of blue and white checked tablecloths that Allegra had provided as a ground cover and watched with undisguised curiosity as Colin and Wellington met, shook hands, and began an intense discussion about she knew not what. Zeebo joined them a moment later, and the animated conversation continued.

Zeebo, as he usually did, tried to take charge of the situation at one point, holding up his hand authoritatively. Wellington spoke heatedly, apparently very angry about something, and even the smooth-tongued Zeebo was compelled to back down and let the man have his say. But Colin broke in and began a long explanation of some kind, quelling Wellington's anger and stimulating his curiosity at the same time. Whatever he was saying seemed to charm the two men into rapt attention. Wellington cooled off visibly, and by the time Colin had finished speaking, they were all laughing heartily and clapping each other on the back. Sabrina sighed anxiously, waiting for Colin to return with an explanation.

But when he found her again, though he was beaming with satisfaction, he was totally reticent about whatever had just taken place.

"Come on," she cajoled. "Tell me. What did he want?"

"Well . . ." he teased, settling down on the cloth and putting down his plate, "it seems that Mr. Wellington is still very interested in *Lady in Flight*." Sabrina plunked down on the grass, her face changing rapidly. "So interested," Colin continued, "that he's reconsidered his price." He took a sip of wine, swallowing slowly to savor its flavor.

"And?" she jumped on him avidly. "What did you tell him?"

"The truth," he answered simply.

"Which is?" She was thoroughly confused, hanging on his reply to make things clear.

"That I'll think about it."

She gave him a fishy look, knowing that he wasn't telling her all of it. "Out with it, Colin. What's going on?"

"Later. Besides, it's nothing definite. Let's just enjoy the day."

She let it go at that, knowing better than to press him. The wind rustled through the trees, creating an atmosphere of peaceful calm. He took a long, slow breath, reveling in the fresh air, and she followed his example, letting the glorious setting have its effect on her.

All around them, the Mangia Society members were doing exactly the same thing. The meadow buzzed with pleasant conversation and obvious enjoyment of the setting and the wonderful food. A butterfly fluttered by, stopping to rest on the dark green bottle of wine that sat upright in its holder, and Sabrina studied its brilliant colors. It remained poised for a moment and then flew off, disappearing behind a cluster of daisies.

They discovered as they ate that Allegra had planned the feast with her usual clever sense of balance. The pungent sausage was the perfect foil after the creamy vichyssoise, and the fish dumplings were equally complemented by the tangy sauce. Even the pristine elegance of the veal was offset by the woody flavor of the wild rice.

Colin groaned with elaborate pleasure when he had licked the last of the dark chocolate from the pot de crème cup. "Do people in France eat like this every day?" he asked languidly.

"I don't know," Sabrina answered. "But if they don't, then I feel sorry for them. A country based on cuisine like this can't go wrong."

"I'll drink to that!" Veronica sauntered by, and she

raised her wine glass gaily as she heard Sabrina's last remark. She sat down to join them for a moment. "Are we going to get started on the fossil hunt soon?" she asked. "I think it's a good idea, before everyone becomes too hopelessly sated with food."

Colin nodded in agreement. "Shall you make the announcement?" he asked Sabrina. "Or should I?"

Before Sabrina could decide, Veronica was banging a fork against her glass as she stood up and commanded the attention of the group.

"Listen, everyone!" she called out, her clear, strong voice ringing out across the meadow. "We have a surprise for you! There's more to this picnic than just the food, as magnificent as it is."

The Mangia Society slowly came to order, quieting down and waiting to hear what she had to say.

"In just a few minutes, we'll be hunting down a dinosaur!"

This was met with curious laughter and surprise, and before reaction to her outlandish statement got out of hand, she was explaining about the fossil in a lucid and convincing manner. Sabrina listened with interest, even though she already knew the whole story, because she was grateful that Veronica was leaving out the part about where the original fossil had been found. She didn't want *Lady in Flight*'s curious history to become common knowledge. It was just too odd.

"So you see," Veronica concluded, "we're looking for an actual missing link." Excitement rippled through the group as people began to understand the importance of the search. She motioned to Colin, who stood up obligingly. "This is Dr. Colin Forrester," she announced. "He discovered the only known fully-preserved fossil of the animal—which from this moment on we will call Roger."

"Roger?!" Colin was nonplussed. "Why Roger?"

"Short for rogericus," she smiled. "Just trying to add a little human interest."

"Fair enough." Colin faced the crowd of people and addressed them with good humor. "First of all," he said, "I'm going to pass out these sketches so that you all know what to look for." Allegra began distributing the pieces of paper as he continued, and the group examined them with growing interest. "We are now sitting in the middle of what used to be a riverbed. It dates back ten million years." Fascinated faces looked up, and he launched enthusiastically into his explanation. "We'll be going down the mountain methodically," he said, "and it will be like going back in time. The further down we go, the older the evidence will be."

"Sounds like a time machine," Zeebo remarked wryly.

"That's exactly what it is," Colin returned persuasively. "But it's right in front of our eyes, if we'll just look for it." His fervor was contagious, and his audience grew excited. A wave of anticipation spread through the group as he outlined the procedure they would follow.

Veronica turned to Sabrina, a tiny smile on her face. "That's quite a guy you've got there."

"Do you think so?" Sabrina looked up, surprised.

"Of course. Knock it off, Sabrina. I can see you're falling in love with him. The only reason you won't admit it is that you're stubborn."

"Stubborn?" Sabrina repeated. "He's the stubborn one, not me."

Veronica nodded complacently. "Spoken like a true stubborn. Listen, if you're both stubborn, then one of you is going to have to make the first move. And it might as well be you." She smiled encouragingly.

"Veronica," Sabrina tried to look stern, "when did you become an expert on my love life?"

Veronica was never easily swayed, and she wasn't now. "I'm just making a suggestion," she said. "But you know I'm right."

Sabrina thought about that as Colin finished his speech. Was she actually falling in love with him? Oddly enough, it hadn't even occurred to her. She had been too busy pushing the possibility away, and focusing instead on what she thought were the differences between them. Unaccountably, the image of Colin standing at the edge of the mountain and looking back in time returned to her. He had been filled with vision then, and suddenly she realized that it was a vision he carried with him all the time.

But love? Sabrina had always thought of love as something very grand and earth-shattering, something that would give her the same kind of awesome thrill that a timeless work of art did. Her feelings for Colin were nothing like that, nothing at all. They were a crazy jumble of emotions that made no sense—a rushing sense of warmth, instinctive defiance, helpless passion, growing tenderness, and a vague need to . . . to prove herself to him. Why? She frowned deeply, lost in thought as the mountain breeze ruffled her hair. Because she respected him. There. It was really very simple, but it surprised her nevertheless. She had felt respect, even adulation, for her first art teacher, and for her parents, who had always lived without the fetters of salaried jobs. Now she felt a similar respect for Colin Forrester. And what was more, she found herself wanting it from him as well.

As he wound up his lecture, holding his audience enthralled, Sabrina stared at him with new understanding and felt almost shy. Looking down at the grass, she wondered avidly how he felt about her. She knew that he found her appealing but she was wise enough to know that, ultimately, that was not enough. Did Colin see her as the serious and dedicated woman she was? She didn't know.

"Okay, everyone," Colin was finishing up, and Sabrina snapped out of her reverie. "I'll pass out hammers and magnifying glasses and then you're on your own."

The crowd began to break up into small groups, and after picking up the tools that Colin was distributing, they spread out in all directions like kids on a camp outing. A few stayed behind to help Allegra clear up debris from the picnic, and this was accomplished with her usual brisk efficiency. Sabrina hung back as Colin answered questions from the group that had gathered around him, feeling rather like a coed waiting for a distinguished professor after class. He remained the center of attention for over fifteen minutes, and by the time he was ready for her, some of the fossil hunters were already returning with samples to show him.

He examined each one patiently, shaking his head each time. "Sorry," he smiled to the first group. "That's just an oddly shaped rock. There's no fossil in it at all." A minute later, he was saying to another group, "What is this thing? Turning over in his hand the object they had brought him, he added, "It looks like a part from an old car." And before long, he was explaining to the third overly enthusiastic team that the leaf they had produced was very recent— twentieth century, in fact. He sent them off again with a word of encouragement, but Sabrina could see that he was becoming a little exasperated.

"How's it going?" she asked, coming up behind him.

"Well . . . they are an enthusiastic bunch, aren't they?" He smiled. "Let's go. I want you to show me where you got that hunk of limestone."

Grateful for the chance to avoid thinking about the turbulent jumble of feelings she had just experienced, Sabrina started off across the meadow. "It's not too far from here," she said. "That's why Allegra and I picked this spot for the picnic."

"I see," he answered, raising an eyebrow. "So there is a method to your madness."

"Always." She spoke almost sharply, and he took her hand, giving it a playful squeeze. She hid the little tremor that his touch had caused and took him to the road at the other side of the mountain. They walked for several minutes, stepping carefully over the rocky decline. Finally they came to a construction area where a new patch of road was being paved, and saw a bulldozer parked off to the side.

"We're close," she said, her hand tightening in his as her eyes scanned the rocky wall in front of them.

Colin's keen eyes followed hers. "This rock is easily two hundred million years old," he murmured, frowning. "But not old enough. It's extremely weathered, though," he added after a moment.

They walked slowly along the newly paved road until they reached a huge expanse of stone that was wedged into the hill.

"There!" she cried, pointing. "That's it!" She ran over to it, nodding in confirmation. "You can see the opening here where they blasted the piece out for me," she added, climbing up for a closer look.

Colin followed slowly, his eyes still scanning the entire area. He peered into the opening and shook his head.

"What is it?" she asked anxiously. "Don't you believe me? I'm positive this is the place."

"Of course I believe you," he answered, surprised. "That's just the problem." He climbed up next to her and used his hammer to explore the edge of the boulder where it fit into the hillside. Dust and segments of rock flew into the air, making a small pile at their feet. At last he stopped and looked into the dent he had just formed. "This is not part of the mountain," he announced flatly, pushing another shower of debris away. "Look here." She stared, but saw nothing unusual. "Don't you see?" he asked. "The limestone is buried in the mountain, but it's not part of it."

Sabrina still did not understand. All she saw was a huge boulder jutting out of the mountain. What was so extraordinary about that?

"It's an erratic," he sighed, stepping back down. "I knew it."

She waited expectantly for him to explain, but he did not. "What's an erratic?" she asked finally, trying to be patient.

"It means it's irregular. It doesn't come from this area. It's a fluke."

"Then how did it get here?" she asked, bewildered.

"It came from Canada," he said, shaking his head. "Just as I thought." Reaching out his hand, he helped her down onto the road. "It's just an oversized rock."

"Well . . . well, maybe there are others like it around here. Where there's one, there's likely to be another, isn't that—"

He stopped her, still shaking his head dispiritedly. "I doubt if there are any others in this area. But there could be some scattered between here and the original spot in Canada where this thing came from. And that's what I need to see—the original spot. This is a red herring." As if to underline his conviction, he looked off to the north, toward Canada.

Sabrina was still in the dark, and she felt that he either assumed she knew what he was talking about, or didn't think she would understand if he explained it. She remembered her fear that he did not take her seriously enough, and decided to test it right there.

"Colin," she said firmly. "If this rock is from Canada, then would you please tell me how it ended up here, embedded in this mountain?" She looked at him intently, and suddenly he smiled.

"I'm sorry," he said gently. "I'm so caught up in this thing that I'm not making any sense." He took her hand and paused. "Remember what I told you before about the glaciers that swept through this area?" She nodded. "Well, one of them came down from the Arctic Circle about . . . oh, eleven thousand years ago. And during the ride, it picked up a lot of debris and incidental items along the way." He looked up at the rock. "This rock was one of the passengers." He led her over to a ledge and sat down. "You can call off the search," he finished dejectedly. "Our missing link isn't here."

She started to say something, but he cut her off.

"Please, Sabrina, just call it off. Go on," he added, nodding in the direction of the meadow. "I'll be with you in a minute. I just want to chip some samples from the limestone to bring back with me." He picked up the hammer and walked back to the boulder.

"Colin," she said, coming up behind him. "Maybe you can find the place where the glacier came from. Maybe you could follow its footprints, so to speak, and trace it back to its original source." She looked up at him hopefully. "Maybe?"

He gazed at her, a new look of wonder and happiness written on his features. "Sabrina!"

"What?" She looked at him anxiously. "What did I say?"

"That's exactly what I'm going to do! How did you know?"

"Really?" She could hardly believe it.

He jumped down and put his arms around her. "Go and tell everyone that the search is off. And as for me . . ." His eyes lit up with excitement. "I'm going on a little trip."

"A trip?" she asked suspiciously. "Or an expedition?"

"Both!" he replied ecstatically. "Both."

Still brimming with excitement, he shooed her away and went back to the rock, chipping away samples to take with him. Sabrina retreated, wondering exactly how he was going to follow the path of a glacier, but figuring that he must know what he was talking about.

Colin hammered at the rock, wondering if any more fossils might be embedded there. There was no time to find out. It would take hours to explore it fully, and he didn't have the proper tools. But this hunk of stone had already yielded something very surprising, and he was only sorry that it had come from so far away.

"Damn!" he muttered, still frustrated at the twist of events. Collecting his samples, he finally stepped down from the boulder and turned to leave. He took a few steps on the new road, when a sudden loud cracking sound emanated from the place where he had been hammering, making him jump back in alarm.

He turned, astonished, and watched incredulously as the solid mass of rock broke apart, letting a huge chunk fall from the hillside. It landed with a crash and splintered into a thousand pieces, a small cloud of dust rising from the debris.

"My God," he said in awe. "The thing is weathered almost to death." He watched as a few more pieces fell, scattering on the ground. "And this is the stone she carved that statue from?" he asked doubtfully. He shook his head pessimistically as he headed back up the mountain. "Poor Sabrina. I'll have to tell her." He shook his head again, letting out a long sigh. "But I know just what she'll say."

Chapter Nine

❧

"Hold that pose! That's it. Perfect, Ms. Melendey!" The photographer focused his camera on Sabrina as she smiled prettily, standing in front of the lengthy tyrannosaurus. Her hair flowed freely around her shoulders, and she wore a new white silk dress with a zigzag hem. The flash blinded her for an instant as the photographer snapped the picture to commemorate the opening of the new exhibit at Lloyd's. Behind her, the main floor was gaily festooned with banners and balloons, and the invited guests milled around, sporting well-tailored suits and elegant but simple dresses.

A local congressman tried to gain the attention of the photographer by pretending to joke with two of the Neanderthal mannequins in the window. "I'm sorry," he said with mock gravity to the inert caveman. "But you can't park your dinosaur here. This is a no parking zone. If you leave him here, he might be towed."

The jest was met with laughter from several of the assembled dignitaries, and someone suggested that the Democratic donkey should be replaced by a dinosaur. This was immediately countered by the notion that the Republican elephant should be replaced by a mastodon. Finally Sabrina implied that all politicians should be symbolized by Neanderthals, and her remark was met with good humor and a tactful change of subject.

Arthur Wellington, in his element at such functions, was busy shaking hands all around the room. When he encountered Sabrina after her session with the photographer, he congratulated her vigorously and led her over to a glittering group in the corner.

"I want you to meet some important people," he announced grandly.

Sabrina smiled and shook hands with Heather Gentree, a silver-blonde woman in her sixties who looked very shrewd and very rich, and her two colleagues, Edgar and Cecil Barlow.

"Ah," Heather Gentree said coolly, looking Sabrina up and down. "You're the talented new artist I've been hearing about. I was at that auction, you know, and I was most impressed. If I had known more about you then, I would have surely outbid that young man who bought your sculpture."

"That young man," Wellington interjected, "was Colin Forrester."

Ms. Gentree pursed her lips and frowned for a moment. "Whom did you say?" she inquired.

"Colin Forrester," Edgar Barlow said dryly. "The paleontologist."

"Forrester . . . Forrester," the woman repeated, trying to jar her memory. "Oh, yes. Wasn't he the one who was bitten by a dinosaur?"

"That's him," Sabrina assured her, holding back a smile.

"Quite an amusing story, I'm sure." The woman's eyes sparkled wryly for a moment. "So, this Mr. Forrester is also a collector of art."

"Not exactly," Wellington said. "His interests in the sculpture were more scientific than artistic, I'm afraid."

Sabrina gulped, afraid that the full story would come out, but Ms. Gentree did not seem at all interested. "Whatever his interests are," she announced, raising a thin eyebrow, "he acquired a very fine piece of work. It captured the very essence of the form, my dear," she added, turning to Sabrina.

"Thank you," Sabrina answered softly.

"Tell me," Ms. Gentree went on after studying the artist for a moment, "have you been very busy this week? My art representative has been trying to get in touch with you, but says there hasn't been any answer."

Sabrina blanched. The truth was that she had been so busy with the Lloyd's displays that she hadn't opened any of her mail or checked her answering machine for messages. "Uh . . . no—I mean yes," she stammered. "What I mean is—"

"I understand, my dear. That's quite all right." Heather Gentree turned to the two men standing next to her. "When one becomes successful, it is often difficult to grasp the sudden, intense interest of others for one's work." She turned back to Sabrina. "I'll come right to the point. I'm interested in some of your other available works, and I'd like to talk to your agent about them."

"My agent?" Sabrina gulped. She didn't have an agent. It appeared that she would have to get one, and soon.

"I understand you've been hoarding your paintings," Ms. Gentree continued with lively interest.

"Really?" Cecil Barlow asked brightly. "How eccentric of you."

"Not at all," Ms. Gentree cut in smoothly. "It's very wise. My third husband always used to swear by supply and demand. Of course, a small supply and a large demand is the ideal combination, and that's what this young lady has been able to attain."

Sabrina tried to look pleasantly grateful for the compliment, but her heart was pounding and her eyes were shining with excitement. She barely knew what to say, and was relieved when Arthur Wellington tactfully extracted her from the group, explaining that there were other people he wanted to introduce her to.

He led her to the other side of the floor where they could talk privately for a moment, and Sabrina saw that no one else was around.

"I was telling a white lie just now," he admitted. "I just wanted you to see for yourself what a commotion that auction has caused among serious collectors."

She looked at him in astonishment.

"Don't you understand?" he persisted. "Your work is in great demand now. That auction has been the number one topic in the art world all week long. *Lady in Flight* is as famous as Grandma Moses. Yesterday I received two calls from two different agents who wanted to know if you were still available. And just this morning I got a call from Schumaker's gallery. They want to do a showing of just about everything you've got."

Sabrina was speechless. She had known, of course, that the auction would be a turning point for her, and she had looked forward to it for a very long time. But this! The reaction it had generated was beyond her wildest dreams.

"I suggest strongly that you get yourself an agent before you do anything," he said sternly. "In the meantime—in case you don't know it already—I called Colin Forrester this morning and offered him another five thousand for *Lady in Flight*." He grimaced. "That man is awfully stubborn. He's got something up his sleeve, but he can't fool me." Then he smiled craftily. "However, I don't give up easily, and I've got a few cards to play myself. I sent Zeebo over to talk to him, acting on my behalf. If Colin doesn't come across, I'll at least make sure that he doesn't lay a hand to that beautiful piece of work. Of that you can be sure!" He congratulated her again on the displays and then left her, going back to mingle with the guests.

Sabrina was completely stunned, though she also felt a tiny but distinct sense of relief. She put a hand to her forehead, trying to absorb it all. Colin had run off last night after returning to the city, telling her only that he was taking another trip, this one up to Canada. He had dropped her off at her loft without a word, and had zoomed off in his truck like a man on a mission. She had tried to call him at his apartment all night, but there was no answer, and she concluded that he hadn't gone home. Had he been at the museum all night? Doing what?? She strongly suspected that whatever he was up to had to do with *Lady in Flight*, and that he had known about it all along. He had been very secretive about it at the picnic yesterday, and even Arthur Wellington seemed to know more about it than she did. And Zeebo! How was he mixed up in all this? She shook her head wearily, feeling like a kid left out of the ball game.

"Always the last to know," she mumbled to herself as a new group of people came over to meet her.

Several minutes later, Zeebo strolled in, splendidly dressed in a dazzling navy suit with a plaid bow tie. "Ah, Sabrina," he said calmly when he saw her. "I've been looking for you."

She didn't hide her surprise at seeing him in his conventional attire, and stared at him with frank amusement.

"What's the matter, love?" he asked. "Haven't you ever seen a man in a suit before?" He turned around, modeling it for her.

"A man, yes. You, never," she chortled, looking him up and down.

"You see a new man before you," he announced dramatically. "I have finally decided on a vocation." He pulled out a bunch of newly-printed business cards and handed her one.

She scrutinized it and looked up in surprise. "You?" she said. "An agent?"

"Yes, me," he replied matter-of-factly. "And guess who my first client is?"

She didn't have to think long. "Me?"

"You!" He gave her a smug smile. "It's the perfect profession for me, you know. After all, I know all the right people, especially the ones with money. And, you have to admit, I know the art scene as well as anyone."

"That's very true," she agreed.

"Actually, it was Arthur Wellington's idea. He suggested it yesterday at the Mangia Society picnic, and I had to agree with him that I'd be simply fabulous at it." He beamed. "So, if you'll just give me the key to your loft, I'll get started."

"You want my key?" she asked warily. "What for?"

"I don't own a gallery yet, love. I already have several customers who are interested in buying an original Melendey, and you've got all those paintings sitting in your loft." He frowned. "Haven't you heard about all the interest?"

"I just learned about it from Arthur a few minutes ago," she confessed. "I—I haven't been available all week. I was just so busy—"

"Never mind," he interrupted, holding up a hand. "I'll take care of all that from now on. You need me, Sabrina. Tell me something. You haven't been opening your mail again, have you?"

"Or answering my messages," she admitted.

"Well, don't worry about it. I'll take care of all that from now on." He waved a hand, dismissing the details.

She looked up then and saw Colin striding toward them through the crowd. He looked oddly disheveled, but was obviously in good spirits.

"Colin!" Sabrina exclaimed. "What are you doing here? I thought you'd be on your way to Canada by now."

His casual camping attire contrasted strangely with Zeebo's suit, and he looked as though he hadn't had much sleep. "Are you all right? You look terrible," she said with concern.

"Maybe," he admitted cheerfully, "but I feel pretty good."

He and Zeebo exchanged a conspiratorial look, which was not lost on Sabrina.

"I assume," Zeebo said to Colin meaningfully, "that you completed that little project we discussed yesterday?"

Colin nodded. "It wasn't exactly little, but yes, I finished—about an hour ago."

Sabrina looked back and forth between the two of them. "What's going on?" she asked.

Colin looked at Zeebo, who immediately backed away. "I think that's my cue to leave," he announced, marching off to leave them alone. Sabrina stared after him and turned back to Colin.

"What was that all about?" she asked.

"Nothing," he said unconvincingly. He was beaming, his face inexplicably radiant for a man who had had no sleep. "Sabrina . . ." He waited for a second and she looked at him expectantly.

"Yes?"

"Sabrina," he repeated. "I—I have two questions for you."

She waited patiently, but he said nothing. "What is it, Colin?"

He took a deep breath. "Would you believe me," he started slowly, "if I were to tell you that your statue is in grave danger of disintegrating?"

Her patience vanished. "Of course not," she said testily.

He nodded seriously. "I was afraid you wouldn't."

"We've been through all that before, Colin," she sighed. "I really don't want to hear it."

"But, Sabrina—"

"No," she insisted, holding up a hand. "Forget it. Is that what you came down here to tell me?"

"Partly. You don't understand. I have to tell you what I saw yesterday. I didn't want to tell you then, but now it doesn't matter, because—"

"If it doesn't matter, then I don't want to hear about it," she repeated firmly. "I mean it, Colin."

He threw up his hands. "Okay, fine. Great. Just forget it."

"Thank you. I will." She paused to emphasize her words, but then she smiled. "Now what was the other question?"

"What? Oh, that. Well, never mind that now," he said tartly. "You're obviously in no mood to listen to reason."

"Colin . . ." Her hands touched his arms, and his eyes melted. "Let's not argue now. Not just before you have to leave."

"You're right," he said, his eyes caressing her face, despite his mood. "I guess I'll see you when I get back."

"Have a safe trip," she whispered.

"I will." He leaned down and kissed her gently.

"Colin?"

"What?"

"What was the second question you wanted to ask me?"

He smiled. "Tell you when I get back." He kissed her again, holding her close for a long moment, and then he left, disappearing into the crowd.

Sabrina watched him with a mixture of curiosity and wistfulness. She suspected that she was going to miss him even more than she had imagined.

Chapter Ten

The cold, wet clay felt comfortingly familiar to Sabrina as her hands kneaded it patiently that afternoon. The routine, simple task seemed to represent a return to reason, a return to the solace that her work always brought. Her world had been turned upside down lately, but there was always this to go back to. Now that the assignment at Lloyd's and the auction were both behind her, she could once again concentrate on the things that really mattered—like her work.

And Colin. It was amazing how quickly he had become a fixture in her life, as if she had known him for years. She remembered how she had dwelt so intently on the differences she had perceived between them, but now those differences didn't seem so important after all. Now that she was used to them, she found that they enlivened things, and even amused her at times. She wasn't sure exactly what would happen between them, but she did know that she was enjoying herself with him more than she ever had with any man. The night in the planetarium shone in her memory like a polished jewel. She knew she would never forget it. He had shared his innermost vision with her then, and she had learned that his passion was not so different from her own.

The work of kneading the clay calmed her, and when at last it was ready, she slapped it into a slab on the flat surface of her work table. A pad lay next to the clay, opened to a sketch she had made in the Adirondacks. Her eyes studied it carefully for a moment, and then she began to work the clay. Her deft fingers formed a large ball, moving quickly over it as her thoughts continued to tumble through her head.

When at last it was ready, she once again studied the sketch in front of her. Her hands moved slowly, planning and thinking with a mind all their own. She looked back and forth from the sketch to the clay, sometimes working for as long as a minute without consulting the drawing at all. She wanted this piece to be quick and dramatic, created with swift, sure strokes. All of the energy inside her flowed to her fingertips, letting her shape the clay with the force of purpose she had commanded.

Sabrina always worked alone. It was not possible to concentrate this intensely when someone else was in the room. When she was inspired, as she was now, the work before her seemed to take over, dominating her and pulling her along on some invisible tide. It would be inconceivable to let the presence of another person interfere with this single-minded energy. And yet, in a crazy way, there was someone in the room with her, and he wasn't bothering her at all. She knew better than to try to stop thinking about him. That would only jar her mood, destroy the flow of her concentration. If Colin could remain so persistently in her thoughts while she was working this well, she had no reason to change it. But it surprised her nevertheless. This had never happened before, and she wondered fleetingly if it would affect her working habits from now on. She had always concentrated solely on her work, never allowing anyone or anything to interrupt her concentration. Any upset or major distraction could be catastrophic, preventing her from giving her best attention to her art.

It had been some time since she had started a new project, but if things went as she hoped, this one would be over as quickly as it had begun. Her goal was to start and complete the piece all in one session—to let it radiate the total energy and sense of design that absorbed her at this moment. If she came back to it again and again, she would lose sight of its force, and its vision would discolor and fade.

The hours passed unnoticed as her skilled hands gradually but fiercely changed the lump of clay into a recognizable, powerful form. The image in the sketch was reproduced in the new medium, but with a sense of drive and purpose that had not been present in her work before. She knew instinctively as her fingers flew that this piece was going to be one of the best she had ever produced.

The expanse of forest looked easy to traverse from Colin's viewpoint high up on the hill, and his spirits rose. By piecing together the available evidence, he had zeroed in on this area above a small, shimmering lake. The two-hour flight had taken him to a small airstrip, and from there he had rented a jeep and headed alone into this remote, timeless region. Off to the left was the lake he sought, and as his eyes caressed the land around him, his mind automatically pieced together its long geological history. Sabrina would love to paint this, he thought. He wondered if she could ever view this land the way he did. Stangely enough, he found that it didn't really matter.

He sat down on a ledge to make notations on his map, and as he began to write he noted something scribbled on the side of the pencil. "This pencil was stolen from Sabrina Melendey's studio," it said, and he laughed. She was right. He had taken it that first day when he had asked her for a tape measure. It was funny how events could intertwine.

He realized that he was sitting here in the middle of this wilderness because a preoccupied woman hadn't answered his letter or phone calls. If she had, he would never have gone to her studio that night, and he would never have seen the fossil.

All of this should have made him happy, but it didn't. Instead, he felt a vaguely disturbing ache. Depression? he asked himself. Is it a letdown after a big discovery? No, he answered honestly, he never felt down during an expedition. This odd feeling had settled into him slowly. He had felt it stirring on the plane that morning, and it had built continually as the trip had progressed.

Trying once again to brush it off, he made his way slowly down into the forest, but the nagging feeling grew even more intense. By the time he reached the lake it had spread over his whole body, and he found that he didn't even have the heart to set up his campsite for the night.

Colin eased his backpack off his shoulders, took off his boots, and walked over to the shore. All around him were the remains of a long-ago time, but he no longer saw the telling details. By now the strange feeling was all-encompassing, and he knew now what it was. It had started back in New York when he had tried to talk to Sabrina. But he somehow hadn't been able to tell her how he really felt. His exhausted mind, a mind that had always been so exacting and scientific, couldn't handle a simple task like telling her how he felt.

Maybe he was afraid. Maybe he didn't want to get hurt. He was tired, he concluded evasively, just too exhausted from working all night to be reasonable. But reason didn't have much to do with love, and a lonely Canadian lake in the wilderness was no place to solve his problem.

He sluggishly began to pitch his tent. It took a long time to get the fire started, and when at last it rose up into a crackling symphony of orange and yellow flames, he sat back feeling completely drained. Why

was this scene so different from any of the others?
How many campfires had he lit by himself, enjoying
the peaceful solitude and listening to the sounds of
animals that made the land come alive? Tonight it all
seemed so distant. He wanted to be anywhere but
here.

Anywhere? No, he realized, it didn't matter where
he was. He'd still feel the same way—like a lone star
in an empty sky. Face it, Colin. For the first time in
your life you feel loneliness. You long for her com-
pany, but you can't admit it. And the sudden
acknowledgment that he was lonely seemed to bring
a natural clearing over his mind and body. He
relaxed, comforted by thoughts of Sabrina.

"My Elf," he murmured gently, and surprised himself by smiling his first smile of the day. The smile
blossomed over his features and all at once he was
aglow in the firelight. In that instant he knew that
what he had wanted to ask Sabrina was not foolhardy
at all, as he had feared. He knew now that he needed
her. And he wanted to tell her immediately, but
couldn't. My kingdom for a telephone, he smiled.
Gazing up at the night sky, his heart beat rapidly as
he conjured her image in his mind. Reluctantly, he
crawled into his sleeping bag inside the tent and
drifted off to sleep, alone.

The first rays of the sun were making their appearance over the World Trade Center, but Sabrina did
not notice. She had been working almost all night,
but she didn't feel tired. She felt exhilarated. Putting
the finishing touches on the sculpture she had just
completed, she stepped back with an impulsive cry
of triumph and surveyed her handiwork proudly. It
captured precisely the savage grace she had wanted
to give it, and it seemed to mirror even more than she
had intended.

Staring back at her, molded expertly from the clay,

was the face of Colin Forrester. The head had a certain nobility, an air of sparkling intelligence, but the eyes were charged with a grandeur that gave it an almost godlike look. It was an honest representation of Colin, yet it seemed to make a clear statement as well. It was obvious, even to the subjective eye of the artist who stood staring at it, that this sculpture had been formed with the deepest of passions. She knew as she looked at it that her hands had been driven by an emotion far stronger than her desire to succeed, or even to create a work of art. The face that looked back at her was tinged with a very special glow. She could not have created that visionary look on the face of any other model. Her portrayal of Colin had been guided by love.

She walked all around it, her critical eye looking for error. But she saw nothing to disturb her, nothing that she wanted to change. She had accomplished her goal. She had forged a single work in one sitting, and it truly reflected the single-mindedness of her intent.

Sabrina caught her breath as she came around to look at the face again. It held an awesome power for her, and she shivered slightly in the empty studio. Suddenly she knew what she wanted to do. She wanted to give Colin this sculpture, to let him have it as a gift. She knew that he still thought she resented his whisking *Lady in Flight* off to the museum without any appreciation of its artistic merit. This gesture would prove that she trusted him to value her work.

Completely satisfied with her decision, she drank a glass of wine to unwind and then crawled into bed. With any luck the clay would harden enough overnight so that she could take it to him the next afternoon. It would still have to be fired properly, but she simply couldn't wait. She wanted him to see what she had done as soon as she could manage it. And she hoped that the emotions which had motivated her to represent him as she had would be as evident to him as they now were to her.

Colin awoke at the break of dawn after a sound sleep. His mellow sadness of the night before was gone, replaced by a sunny positive feeling. The fresh breeze on his face was invigorating as he lit the fire and made a cup of coffee that tasted uncommonly good. Everything seemed right today, and he intended to make the most of it.

He always made important decisions in the morning, but this particular morning he had made the best decision of his life. He wondered what Sabrina would say. As he finished breakfast his eyes took in the expanse of rock and terrain that surrounded the lake in front of him. Somewhere out there, perhaps even in the lake itself, were the remains of a creature that had already made a permanent dent in his life, personally as well as professionally. But he was too impatient to let the time slip away in daydreaming. There was work to be done and he had no intention of missing the afternoon flight back to civilization. If he got lucky, he could be back in time for a dinner with Sabrina. Without a second thought, he gathered his hammer and magnifying glass and walked toward the edge of the lake, noting the different rock formations that told a story about the history of the region. His professional eyes worked like a movie projector. Each layer of rock took him further back in time, going deeper and deeper in search of the right era.

But he soon found that every approach was a dead end, and after a few hours he began to realize the futility of his search. It was a needle in a haystack, he thought as he walked down and sat by the lake. Taking up a handful of pebbles, he began skimming each one across the water, admiring the patterns they made. Each one made a tiny plunk before disappearing, and the idle game amused him for a while.

But soon he grew tired of it, dropping the remaining stones into a little pile in front of him. He folded his arms, contemplating his next move as he stared at the lake. The utter silence was unsettling, and he reached down again to play with the small pile of pebbles. His hand touched one and he picked it up, glancing down at it carelessly. His face froze in sudden recognition. It was no pebble that he held, but an ancient shell. A shell that dated exactly from Roger's time. And it was almost all the proof he needed.

Somewhere, right where he sat, there had to be another Roger. His heart began to beat rapidly. With no time to lose, he began frantically sifting through the sand and gravel a few feet at a time. His eyes lit up once more as he found another shell from that era. And a few minutes later two more appeared. Two hours passed as he worked relentlessly, methodically sorting through the mass of ancient debris. He never stopped to rest, moving quickly and surely, confident that this search would have a triumphant end. He was hungry and tired, but he didn't want to stop, not now.

But at last, utterly exhausted, he fell on his stomach, and let his arms flop straight out in front of him, so that his hands met with the icy coldness of the lake water. His fingers hit something hard, and he scraped the sand to pick it up. It was only another shell. No, it wasn't a shell. It was a tooth. A tooth! His eyes widened as he scrambled to sit up and examine it. Yes, there was no doubt about it. It was from another Roger!

With a whoop that echoed through the area, he jumped up and danced an impromptu jig, holding his precious evidence in his hand. There would have to be a whole expedition organized for the summer, and now he had the evidence to justify such an expedition. Carefully placing the tooth in a clear bag, he zipped it into his pocket and patted it solicitously.

Then he took out his pencil and pinpointed the exact spot on the grid map. He looked at Sabrina's pencil once more.

With a little smile, he fished out a scrap of paper and made a little flag. The pencil hovered over it for a second, and then he wrote, "The Melendey Expedition" on it. Rolling the flag tightly around the end of the pencil, he dug a hole in the sand where he had found the fossil and buried the pencil and its banner.

His smile broadened. With luck, he would be back in time to have dinner with her.

Sabrina checked the clay to see if it had hardened sufficiently overnight. Like a rock. She smiled, satisfied. She looked at the clock. It was well past midday. She had worked very, very late, but it was worth it. She had still been able to get a full eight hours of sleep, and she felt fresh and rested. Colin would be back soon and she wanted to surprise him with her new work, to let him see without words how she felt about him. Her only problem would be lugging it over to the museum.

She managed to get the heavy piece onto the elevator, remembering how they had moved *Lady in Flight* only a short time before. The story of my life, she laughed to herself, coming out of the building and hailing a cab.

She entered the museum through the front, carefully holding onto the sculpture as she made her way through the crowds. On the fourth floor, she passed through the Hall of the Dinosaurs on the way to Colin's office. As she went by the large exhibit hall she glanced over at the seymouria. A huge crowd had gathered at that end of the exhibit and she couldn't see anything through the crush of people. There must be a new display there, she surmised. She dodged the crowd and stepped into Colin's office, passing an assistant who looked curiously at the sculpture and then smiled in recognition. Sabrina put it down gently on his desk, and after scribbling a short note, she turned to leave. But something in the corner caught her eye. It was tall, it was mysterious, and it was draped in a large white sheet. *Lady in Flight*, most likely. She ventured over to take a look at it. She lifted the covering confidently, but her hand froze in midair when she saw what was there. Completely stunned, she gazed at the work in front of her. It was *Lady in Flight*, all right—in bronze.

Her hand trembled as she recalled something Colin had once said. Suddenly she realized what it was he had been working on all night long. He had been making a copy of her statue. She stared at it in awe. Copying dinosaur bones was one thing, but this! She was shocked. And yet as she studied it, a slow feeling of triumph came over her. He had done this for her. The whole night after the trip to the Adirondacks while she had slept, Colin had been creating this.

Her fingers ran slowly, intimately over the curves of the statue, caressing it as if it were something even greater than what she had made. The smooth texture of the metal was a sharp contrast to the coarseness of the limestone. She couldn't help seeing that bronze gave the form more luster and presence. It was not the same as the original, but it had a beauty all its own.

Her fingers continued to follow its curves around to the back, when suddenly she stopped as she felt instinctively that something was not right. There was a long fissure going up the small of the *Lady's* back. Sabrina held her breath as she walked around to look at it. Sure enough, a long, deep crevice ran the length of the back, scanning the set of protrusions.

It was easy enough to put two and two together. Someone—or something—had cracked the original, and Colin had copied it. But she simply couldn't believe that he had deliberately damaged her work.

Not now, after everything that had happened.
Sabrina realized with a glowing surge of certainty
that she trusted him. It didn't matter if he understood
the ins and outs of everything she did as an artist; he
respected her, and that was enough. More than
enough. As she sat staring at the ugly gash, she
remembered he had tried to tell her that something
like this could happen. She hadn't listened. She had
been stubborn and unreasonable, and now . . . she
was looking at the handiwork of her own failing.

She had so much to ask him, so much to tell him.
And as for *Lady in Flight* . . . where was the original,
anyway? Her eyes darted frantically around the room
looking for it, but it was nowhere among the old
bones and fossils that were scattered all around. She
ran back out into the hall looking for one of Colin's
assistants, but they had disappeared. She looked
around impatiently, hoping to find a guard, but all
she saw were the huge dinosaurs and glass-cased
exhibits. The crowd continued to throng around the
seymouria, and she was tempted to go and see what
was so interesting when she suddenly saw Colin
coming out of the elevator. He was still wearing his
camping outfit, and he didn't see her as he marched
past the crowd.

She tried to catch his attention, but his mind
seemed to be focused on something else, and he
looked unaccountably happy, as if he were hoarding
a wonderful secret. She ran up behind him as he
stepped into his office, but stopped short, staring at
his back, as he caught sight of the sculpture sitting on
his desk.

Colin walked slowly around it, and she caught her
breath as his profile came into view. She sank back
into the shadows, watching the tender, bemused
expression on his face. She was dying to rush inside
and ask him about *Lady in Flight*, but she dared not
interrupt as he quietly surveyed her portrayal of him.

After several tremulous moments, he sat on the edge of his desk, his back to her, and picked up the phone to dial a number. "Yes," he said into the receiver, "I'd like to send a dozen—no, make that two dozen— roses. . . . Yes. Colin Forrester, Museum of Natural History. . . . That's right." There was a pause, and then he gave Sabrina's name and address. "The card? Oh, just have it say . . ." Sabrina held her breath. "Just have it say, 'I love you.' "

He hung up gently and continued to stare at the sculpture. Sabrina could not see his face, but an idea had come to her, and suddenly she did not want him to see her there. Silently she slipped away and headed toward the elevator, her eyes shining with anticipation.

Colin sat down at his desk and shook his head several times. He had never felt so touched, so honored, in his life. Sabrina was always full of surprises, but now he found that he was getting used to them. She was full of life, full of joy.

Suddenly he started as he realized that a full thirty minutes had gone by, and he had been daydreaming like a schoolboy about Sabrina. The stack of mail and messages on his desk reminded him that there was work to be done. But first and foremost he had to take care of the precious fossil he had found.

An hour passed quickly as he became absorbed in his work. After returning several calls and opening his mail, he went down the hall to get a drink of water. When he came back, he discovered to his surprise that a bouquet of carnations had been delivered, waiting for him on his desk. He frowned. He had distinctly said roses, not carnations, and they were supposed to go to Sabrina, not to him. Couldn't they accomplish such a simple task? Annoyed, he fished out the card. Well, at least they had gotten the message right. The words "I love you" were plainly printed, with no signature.

He debated calling the florist back, but quickly decided against it. He was seized with the desire to see her and couldn't wait for a florist. He would deliver the flowers himself, even if they weren't roses. The red, white, and pink carnations looked very pleasant wrapped in white paper, and their subtle fragrance filled him with promise.

He ran out of the museum and into a cab, giving Sabrina's address to the driver. It seemed to take forever for the cab to wend its way through the traffic to SoHo, but at last they pulled up in front of Sabrina's building. Colin tossed the driver a bill and jumped out. What would he say to her? Would she respond as he hoped? He didn't have time to think about those questions. He took the steps two at a time and knocked, quite out of breath, on her door.

She answered almost immediately, and he blinked in confusion when he saw her. She was barefoot, dressed in her blue and white caftan, her dark hair flowing freely around her sloping shoulders. In her arms nestled two dozen red roses, and his card was still in her hand. In a flash he understood what had happened. They stood staring at each other without a single word.

It was Colin who finally broke the silence. "No one ever sent me flowers before," he said.

"I would have been happy just to get the card," she answered, her voice barely above a whisper.

There was another pause, but this time their faces began to light with a surge of happiness.

"I think this calls for a celebration," she said softly. "Would you like a glass of wine?"

He stepped inside and closed the door behind him. Never had he felt so happy, even though there was still so much to talk about. As he sat down on the rug Sabrina poured two glasses of wine and handed him one. She sat down facing him, crossing her legs in front of her.

"You found something in Canada, didn't you?" she asked, her eyes shining. He sensed that she was temporarily trying to avoid the deeper subject—the one that would involve the two of them—but he understood and let her guide him away from it. He was even a little relieved. You couldn't just burst in on a woman and ask her to marry you.

He nodded. "I found a tooth. From another rogericus. It's back in my office."

Sabrina let out a cry of joy. "A whole tooth? Really? Oh, Colin, that's wonderful!" She held up her glass. "To Roger."

He smiled and nodded. "To Roger. Our old, old friend."

He watched the contours of her face as she drank. She seemed to have grown even more beautiful, and he wasn't sure why. It wasn't simply that she had started to really listen to him, to understand his work for what it was. There was something more, an underlying current of reaction that threatened to swell up and burst within him. During their first week he had taken that reaction and used its energy, channeling it into the feverish lovemaking that had overpowered them both. But now it seemed that even fiery physical expression would not be enough. She was a butterfly to him, an elusive, breathtaking creature always just out of reach. He knew that he *had* to reach her now, had to possess her in a way that no one ever had. If he didn't there would always be an empty, hollow space inside of him that only she could fill.

Her eyes glowed emerald as she smiled, revealing her perfect white teeth, and Colin's heart swelled as he looked at her. He had claimed that he did not believe in magic, but that wasn't true. Sabrina created magic with her slender hands, with the stroke of a paintbrush or the molding of clay. She knew how to create illusion, and to make it so real that it super-

seded the reality. With her special vision, she
portrayed the world around her not as it was, but as it
should be.

"Titania," he whispered. "That's who you are. You
were put on this earth to torment me."

"Titania?" she repeated doubtfully. "What happened to Elf?"

"I've promoted you. From a mere elf to a fairy
queen. You can't object to that."

"No," she whispered, her eyes shining.

Sabrina watched Colin with a new curiosity. She
always looked at faces; faces and hands were her fas-
cination, revealing more about a person than anything else. Yet now he was inscrutable to her. She
had absolutely no idea what he was thinking, and she
wanted to know, wanted to look inside his mind and
read the secrets hidden there. Her approach to the
world was to interpret it, to hold it up to her own private mirror and portray it, but Colin's was to understand it and explore it until he mastered it.

His keen eyes gazed back at her over the rim of
his wine glass, seeming to measure her. The irregular
planes of his face were boldly handsome, defying the
prettified standards of magazine-style beauty with a
powerful masculinity all their own. She had thought
that he was attractive before, but now his profile left
her breathless. Her fingers itched for a pencil to
sketch him again, but she felt that no drawing could
ever capture Colin the way she saw him now.

He finished the wine and leaned back, his lean,
tightly muscled body stretching out leisurely in front
of her. Sabrina's heart quickened as she looked at
him. She already knew that his mere touch could
arouse her immeasurably. Now he could excite her
simply by moving his body in that lazy, leonine way
of his.

"Sabrina," he said gently.

Her heart jumped. His utterance of her name

sounded like a caress. "Will you come here?" he asked.

She moved toward him, her eyes searching his with solemn expectance. How much had changed since she met him! He had come into her life as a nuisance, and now he was her lover, capable of inspiring her deepest emotions. They gazed at each other for a full minute, a minute that lasted for a small eternity. Sabrina did not know that her face was practically glowing, its delicate lines shining fluidly even in the dim light. She knew only that she wanted this man as she had never wanted anything in her life.

She wondered how easily her desire could be read on her face, especially when Colin lifted her chin with one finger and looked at her searchingly. Sabrina raised her eyes to his very slowly, almost afraid of the rising tumble of emotions within her. He took her hands in his, and they lay there like two limp birds, completely under his spell.

"Sabrina," he whispered. His voice sent a thrill coursing through her body, and it was then that she felt her emotions seem to melt, flowing out through her hands and into his. He squeezed very gently, and the yearning trembled right into her fingertips.

She sank into his arms then, her heart fluttering and every nerve ending awake and ready for his touch.

Colin held her easily, letting her softness work its magic against his chest. He felt that he could sit here with her like this forever, stopping only to make love to her when the fever in them swelled. He remembered dimly why they were here—the fossil that had brought them together in the first place. And suddenly it all seemed unimportant. He realized with a sense of wonder that he had found what he wanted right here. If only this elusive, fragile, fairy queen of a woman could stay still long enough to trust him, to believe in him.

She sighed suddenly, a tiny wisp of a sigh.

"What is it?" he asked.

"Colin . . . I . . ."

"Yes?" He sat back and looked at her, trying to read her thoughts. She said nothing more, and whatever she had started to tell him became lost as he kissed her, delving into her petal-soft lips with his tongue. The kiss quickly blossomed, engulfing both of them in its power. He undressed her slowly, removing each item with care and leaving sensuous kisses on each part of her as it became bared. She was vibrant with anticipation by the time he finished, and she lay on the rug with one knee bent and her hair tumbling around her shoulders.

Colin slipped quickly out of his own clothes and stretched out next to her, his eyes raking her naked body with undisguised need. Sabrina reached up with both hands and cupped his head. She could not hide the fact that her hands were trembling, but she didn't care. The tide of love that had started was growing almost unbearable within her.

She kissed him repeatedly, dropping tiny strokes on his neck and his shoulders, and her fingers drew sensitive lines down the hard length of his chest. He responded instantly, closing his eyes for a few moments to relish the sensation. When he opened them, her face was smoky with passion, and he bent to her breasts, teasing them into fullness. His mouth continued its slow, sensual journey until it arrived at the gentle curve of her stomach. Her hands played feverishly in his hair as he followed the delicate line of her thigh, leaving fire wherever he touched her. He moved back up, holding her firmly in his strong arms, and her hands moved restlessly over his legs and his broad back. She wanted something different suddenly, something that would show him exactly how much he meant to her. Struggling beneath his weight, she sat up, her legs stretched out in front of her. He sat up too, looking puzzled, but only for a moment.

Sabrina lifted herself and wrapped her legs around his back so that she was sitting on his thighs. Her small breasts stood only inches from his chest, and they rose and fell with the rhythm of her breathing. She looped her slender arms around his neck and let them hang there, but did not pull him close to her body. Very carefully, without any wasted motion, she shifted so that his hardness was lodged against her.

Colin responded with a hoarse groan. He thrust his hips forward in one powerful motion that joined them together, and Sabrina cried out with pleasure. Then they were only able to move very slowly, almost imperceptibly at times, in order to preserve the angle of their union. Sabrina shuddered violently at the exquisite torment, wanting desperately to clasp him to her and rock wildly above him, but knowing that anticipation would make the final pleasure all the more fulfilling. He explored and probed the interior of her body, not with long, smooth thrusts, but with an inch-by-inch thoroughness that made her tremble.

Sabrina fell forward, her breasts warm against his chest. Her body was flooded with response, and her breaths came in short, uneven sighs that were punctuated by little tremors. She did not think she could last much longer as they continued to move together, and suddenly he turned her over onto the floor with a harsh cry. Her legs remained wrapped around him and his arms were underneath her body, holding her close as he began a driving rhythm that answered and satisfied the tremendous buildup they had created. His movements were now swift and sure, claiming and possessing her. He wanted to possess her this way always, always to have a hold on her free spirit. But since he knew he could not, he put his heart and soul into the one path that was open to him—the physical expression of his love for her.

Sabrina's eyes filled with tears, but she did not stop her frenzied movements. She felt that every cell in her body was crying out to him, giving him everything that she had. Her surrender was complete as she lost herself in his arms. And the urgency of it was painfully poignant as they went to oblivion together and back, their voices mingling to shatter the stillness around them.

"I love you," she cried, astonished to see tears in his eyes that matched her own.

His face was still haggard with passion as he cradled her. "And I love you," he whispered. "I need you, Sabrina. Don't ever leave me."

Her eyes misted. "I won't," she answered softly.

"But—"

"But what?" she prodded gently, nestling against his shoulder.

"What about all our differences? What about *Lady in Flight*? What about—"

"Shhh," she said, placing a finger against his lips. "We're not so different. In fact, I've begun to see how alike we really are. We just have different ways of expressing the same thing."

Encouraged, he smiled a little. It was exactly the same conclusion he had come to. His eyes met hers. "Sabrina, about *Lady in Flight* . . ." He barely knew how to tell her, but she surprised him.

"Oh, I know all about that," she whispered softly.

"You do?" he gaped. Then he frowned. "You know what?" he asked cautiously.

"It cracked. And you copied it. Thank goodness." Her eyes sparkled and she smiled at him. "It looks beautiful, Colin."

He stared at her in awe. "You mean you—"

"I saw it. And it's okay. Really. I think the crack

can even be covered in the bronze." She took his hands and squeezed them for emphasis.

"You mean you don't mind?" His face was flooded with relief. "And I thought you might even blame me." He put his arms around her and she managed a small laugh.

"Don't you think I trust you by now?" she asked plaintively.

He held her shoulders and looked into her eyes. "Do you, Sabrina?"

"Yes," she whispered solemnly. "Now and always."

Her words filled him with promise. "Listen, Titania," he began. "You're not too much of a free spirit to be against settling down, are you?" He paused. "I was afraid you would think it awfully conventional of me, but—"

"Oh, Colin," she sighed. "Don't you trust *me*?"

"Of course I do!"

"My parents have been happily married for years, you know," she reminded him with a slight pout. "Some things are never out of style."

He looked at her radiantly. She waited, but he said nothing, only gazed at her with so much love that at last she said, "The answer to your question is yes."

"Yes?" He looked so startled that she laughed.

"Yes!" she sang out. "Yes, yes, yes, yes, yes!"

They laughed merrily, rolling in each other's arms. "Well, that's good," he gasped, "because that was the second question I was going to ask you yesterday."

"Yesterday? You wanted to ask me yesterday?" Sabrina's heart flooded with happiness. Her joy mingled with his until it became too great to bear, and then they made love again, surrounded by the delicate fragrance of roses and carnations.

If you go to the fourth floor of the Museum of Natural History, you will see a very strange exhibit in the Hall of the Dinosaurs.

It is an exhibit that is quite literally falling apart. And the more it disintegrates, the better it becomes.

Sitting next to the glass-cased seymouria is an original rogericus embedded in the derriere of a sculpture of a female nude. The statue is placed so that the remarkable fossil is easly visible to the viewer. There is always a swarm of people around it, and it is one of the most popular exhibits in the whole museum.

The artist, of course, always wanted her work to be shown in a museum. She never dreamed it would be this one.

But she's very happy just the same.

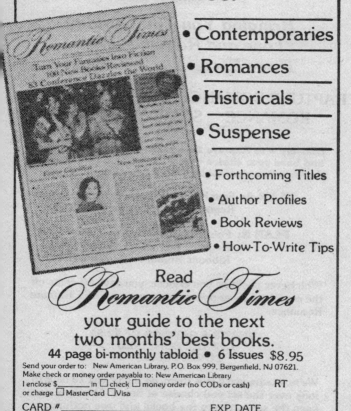

RAPTURE ROMANCE
BOOK CLUB

Bringing You The World of Love and Romance With Three Exclusive Book Lines

RAPTURE ROMANCE   SIGNET REGENCY ROMANCE   SCARLET RIBBONS

Subscribe to Rapture Romance and have your choice of two Rapture Romance Book Club Packages.

PLAN A: Four Rapture Romances plus two Signet Regency Romances for just $9.75!

PLAN B: Four Rapture Romances, one Signet Regency Romance and one Scarlet Ribbons Romance for just $10.45!

Whichever package you choose, you save 60 cents off the combined cover prices plus you get a FREE Rapture Romance.

"THAT'S A SAVINGS OF $2.55 OFF THE COMBINED COVER PRICES"

We're so sure you'll love them, we'll give you 10 days to look over the set you choose at home. Then you can keep the set or return the books and owe nothing.

To start you off, we'll send you four books absolutely **FREE.** Our two latest Rapture Romances plus our latest Signet Regency and our latest Scarlet Ribbons. The total value of all four books is $9.10, but they're yours **FREE** even if you never buy another book.

To get your books, use the convenient coupon on the following page.